I0764655

The Eyes of a Wolf

By Heather McNeil

Wolfwyse Publications
17281 SW Stellar Dr. Sherwood OR 97140

Summary: An orphaned puppy strives to make his mark on the world and bridge the gap between humans and wolves.

Printed in the U.S.A.
Paperback edition

ISBN number: 978-0-615-26170-6

This book is dedicated to my wonderful parents, Mike and Julie. Without you, I would be nowhere.

Also to my grandparents, Jack and Vivian, whose love and enthusiasm helped keep my dream alive.

And to my Grandfather Craig, who wielded a paintbrush of words. Becoming an author was not my desire alone but one we shared. I regret having never met you.

Lastly, to my brother, Craig, who inspired this story.

Acknowledgements

I would like to thank George Herman, Amy Alexander, Lori Ries, Michele Avanti and Marta Turner for sharing with me some very useful information that aided me during the writing process as well as being there to willingly answer any questions I had.

A special thank you goes out to my fourth grade teacher, Dana Miller, who first introduced me to the wonders the world of writing has to offer.

All of my friends and family members, who were willing to lend an ear and help inspire me with their laughter and lively personalities, provided the extra push I needed to pursue and achieve my goals. I am forever grateful for all of you.

Prologue

Midnight folded itself over the Rocky Mountains, veiling everything in a velvet black and silencing the day's noise. The darkness penetrated trees, wound its way through the mountains and made its way onto a small farm situated in the hills. A harvest moon hung above the scene, bright and round as a pumpkin. Cows grazed lazily in the fenced pasture, contentedly chewing the grass. They all looked up as an eerie howl rose above the hills and floated out over the farm. It faded away into chilling silence, echoing through the air. There was no answering call and the cows relaxed and continued grazing.

The sound had come from closer than any of the animals had anticipated- mere yards away, next to the farmhouse. A wolf stood, a soft breeze ruffling the fur around his neck. He temporarily swept the fields with his bright yellow eyes before padding toward the quaint little house. He was large and muscular with his tail held erect and sleek, black fur. He might have been a ghost as he moved about, making absolutely no noise, he wove in and out of trees, heading for the distant building.

He stopped, sniffing the air for a brief moment and, catching a scent, preceded toward the porch. Instead of stepping onto the decrepit platform, he ducked beneath it, walking slowly and with his head bent to avoid scraping the wood above, he made his way under the house. It was damp and uneven here and he had to walk carefully. When he came to a spot where the ground leveled out, he stopped. A few feet away, tucked into a corner, was a gorgeous, female German shepherd dog. She lifted her head as she saw him and wagged slightly. He came closer and gave her face a lick before looking down at her belly.

Eight tiny newborn pups were nestled there, sleeping. The wolf looked at them proudly and gave their mother an affectionate glance. He bent down to sniff them gently and smiled. They were no more than a day old and were already beginning to show signs of the wolfish blood that ran through their veins. He turned a circle and lay down next to the dog; resting his head on his large paws.

Above them, humans could be heard, walking across the floors and going about their business as usual. It began to rain and he was suddenly grateful for the shelter of the little house. The pattering drops lulled his companion to sleep and he watched her as she closed her eyes and began twitching, caught up in a dream.

A small movement caught his eye and he turned his head to identify it. A puppy was curled up a few feet away, shivering. Too far away from its siblings and mother to feel their body heat, it began whimpering pitifully. It was not small and the wolf wondered why his mate had chosen to abandon it. He rose quietly, being careful not to wake the sleeping dog, and approached the pup.

There was not much he could do to help it and

he whined quietly. If his mate had abandoned it, it was probably for good reason. Even so, he found that the little one's cries stabbed at his heart and he was suddenly overcome with sympathy. As gently as he could, he picked it up in his mouth and crawled out from under the house. He trotted up the creaky steps onto the porch and set the puppy down in front of the door. He considered scratching at the peeling paint to get the humans' attention but shook his head. They would find it soon enough.

Taking one last look at the helpless pup before him, he turned around and sped off. In seconds, he was swallowed up by darkness, leaving the puppy alone, its cries echoing against the silence.

Contents

Part 1
The Beginning

Chapter 1
The Unknown

Wind whistled through a dark, menacing forest and gave the trees their voices. Leaves murmuring and branches cackling, they conversed with each other in hushed tones. It was dark and the area lay shrouded in the protective arms of the night. All the secrets of this place- rocks, weeds and puddles- which would normally have appeared sharp and clear, even at night, were fuzzed as though a giant hand had smudged the scene with charcoal.

The eerie stillness of the site was suddenly broken as a dark figure passed through it. The figure made no sound as it traveled across the harsh ground. It came into a patch of moonlight that had filtered through the tree branches and stopped. The figure lifted its head and two yellow eyes flashed in the dark.

Its tongue lolled out of its mouth as its breath drifted in front of it in soft puffs of air. It looked around for a fleeting second and then swiftly broke into a run, disappearing quickly through the trees...

The dog was jerked suddenly from his quick paced dream and regretted it the moment he had done so.

Growling at himself, he lifted his head a fraction to see what had woken him: one of his twitching feet had collided with his water dish, upturning the bowl and completely soaking one corner of his cage. He put his head back on his paws and breathed calmly.

At first, he felt contented to be lying there but then reality caught up with him. He was wet and cold, the metal under him was hard and the stale smell of too many animals hung in the air. He groaned. Here he was again-the same place he always woke to, no matter how magnificent his dreams. He closed his eyes again and for a second, was almost able to go back to sleep.

Again he was disturbed, however as a sharp barking rang out across the room. Normally, he would have been able to ignore it but this was not just any kind of bark; it was a plea for help. His ears twitched anxiously as his head shot up to see what was going on.

It was common for him to see other dogs in this place, in fact, he saw them every day. All he needed to do was glance out of his small cage and there they were, faring no better than he, all in steel kennels identical to his and all with that same oppressed look on their faces. Very rarely they would be taken out for short walks and so every once in awhile he could spot a dog being led via leash down a tiled hall that extended just off to the right of where he sat. There, they would be led through a door and eventually come back all smiles and wags.

There was, however another door and it was situated just across from the dog's cage. Where it led, he hadn't a clue, only that he never wanted to cross its threshold because as far as he knew, there had never been a dog that had entered it and returned.

So it was, as he looked out of his cage he immediately spotted what all the commotion was about. A brown dog was being led, snarling viciously, down this particular hall. She was wearing a muzzle that slightly muffled her frantic barks but even so, her message to the surrounding animals was perfectly audible: "Help!" No one could do anything and the others watched as the bristling female dog was taken through the door and all was quiet for a moment as her barks died away. Then, suddenly, another dog started barking because he had seen a mouse on the floor and the whole atmosphere instantly returned to normal.

The dog sat back down, a fresh wave of remorse splashing over him. So this was life; trapped here in his cage with no human owner to look up to and watching casually as others were taken away to die? He couldn't convince himself of that. There had to be more out there worth living for.

He had overheard stories passed between other dogs about what life was really like. There had been dogs who had actually had owners before they came here and a loving family, too. He could not imagine what it must be like, for he had spent nearly his entire life in this place. He had been very small when he was brought here and the memories of how he had lived then were faded. He could still remember enough to piece together the reason for why he was here, though.

His mother had rejected him. Apparently, she had had too many puppies to nurse properly and rather than risk an entire litter, she had chosen to pick one and ignore it completely. That one had been him. He could faintly remember the warmth of his mother's body and then the coldness of the ground under him. He remembered being moved away from his littermates as he tried to wrestle them and then rolling down a slight dip in the earth. There were these memories and then there were his first memories of where he resided now. He could not remember how he had been brought here but suspected that a human had found him.

He had been marked a reject from the moment he was born. Now here he was and even the humans that came by every now and then didn't want him. They would walk down the aisles and look at animals. More than half of the time they would stop at a particular cage and seem to take a liking to the animal that occupied it. If they did, the animal would eventually be taken out and the human would take it away.

There was a huge difference between *that* exit and a dog being led down a mysterious hall and through a mysterious door. These humans were different from the ones that led a dog to its unknown doom. These humans did not have that solemn, detached air to them; they cared about the one they took with them and there was never a doubt in any animal's mind that any harm would come to them. From that point on, the animal would pledge its unending loyalty to the human that had set it free from this place of outcasts and rejects.

Of course, *he* was still here. No human had ever expressed to him the kind of interest they did in all the others and as a result, he had been here longer than most dogs: from a puppy to an adult.

Perhaps this was the reason why no one seemed to care for him. He was not a puppy anymore and had completely lost his cute, puppyish looks. The puppies were always the first pick and none brought in ever stayed longer than two weeks. So too, with the small dogs and kittens or the ones that had interesting patterns on their fur- he was none of these.

Every once in awhile he would catch a glimpse of his reflection in his water bowl. Compared to the other dogs his age, he was not particularly handsome. His snout was longer than the others' and so were his legs. His front paws were slightly larger than his back paws and he looked much lankier than most of them. There was also something different about his eyes. He couldn't exactly put his paw on it but they were different somehow, maybe it was the shape. They were definitely a different color. Was it yellow? He couldn't really tell. The water was always murky and his image was sometimes disfigured.

He was sitting there, thinking hard, until something interrupted his thoughts- his stomach was growling at him. With a sigh, he stood up and walked cheerlessly over to his food bowl. It had not been refilled recently and all that was left were a few minute bites. At least it was something. He quickly downed the food as he had learned to do. If he ate too slowly the horrible taste would catch up with him.

Licking his snout, he turned back around and froze. There was a human looking at him. He had never received that look from any being in his life. It was fondness. He had seen it before but it had never been directed toward him and he didn't know what to do with himself.

He simply stood there for a shocked second and then the human walked closer until they were just feet apart. The only thing separating them was the steel bars of the dog's cage. Warily, he moved forward, slowly putting one paw in front of the other, until his nose was just inches from the human, who had bent down on hands and knees to get a closer look. The dog took a quick sniff and the scent told him the human was a male. He was small, though. Smaller than most of the humans and so, he concluded, must be a pup. There was a different word that humans used though. After thinking for a split second, the dog remembered it: boy.

The boy had blonde hair and green eyes. He wore a pair of shoes that smelled strongly of the outside world and a dazzling smile.

"Hey," said the human boy gently, "You look so sad here." He poked his finger through the steel bars and the dog's first instinct was to flinch. He reminded himself that every move he made now could determine his future. Gently, he licked the boy's finger. The human's face lit up at the dog's affection.

Suddenly, another human walked over. It was a female; she was much bigger than the boy and obviously an adult. The dog guessed she was the boy's mother. She reached down and put her hand on his shoulder.

"C'mon, honey. You're in the wrong section. We need to be over where the puppies are," she said.

"Never mind, mom. I changed my mind- I want this one!"

The female exhaled sharply through her nose and bent down next to the boy to peer in at the dog. Her brow became furrowed as she looked him over, her eyes taking in his form and scrutinizing it carefully.

"He's so big. I'm sure a dog like that needs a lot of exercise… more than we can give him."

The dog could sense the increased amount of anxiousness the boy was experiencing and he allowed his hopes to rise a little.

"Please, mom," the little human started, "I promise I'll take good care of him. I'll feed him and walk him all by myself." The female seemed to be thinking.

"Well… you promise that I won't have to remind you at all?" She asked.

"Oh yes! I promise!"

"Alright then. Let's go find out what we need to do before we take him home."

Now the anxious aura the boy gave off switched to excitement and joy. He jumped up and practically skipped after the female human as they disappeared down a hall.

The dog had never been so nervous. He paced back and forth restlessly and nearly upturned his water bowl again. He started panting, hoping desperately that the two humans would return to set him free.

A few minutes passed and the dog was about ready to start howling when he saw them coming back down the aisles toward him, being followed by another human, who the dog quickly realized was one of the employees here.

They stopped at his cage and then the employee asked, "This one?"

The female nodded, "Yes, that's the one. Now,

exactly what breed is he?"

The employee bit his lip, "We're not really sure. He's some kind of a mix between a German shepherd and a… hmmm… husky, maybe. But you do understand that, because he's not a pure breed, he won't be able to compete in any dog shows or anything, right?"

"Yes, yes, of course," said the female.

"Okay, then." The employee bent down and unlocked the dog's cage. As soon as the door was open, the dog stepped out onto the hard, cement floor, glad to be out of the confined space. The employee pulled a short leash out of his pocket and laced it around the dog's neck. As he did so, the boy and the female were talking.

"Are you sure you want this one?" asked the adult.

"Of course!" Answered the boy definitely.

"You seem so sure though, I thought you would have liked a smaller dog, one that you can hold."

"Well," the boy thought for a second. "I *did* but this dog is special."

"Special? He looks like any normal German shepherd to me, except that… he's not really a puppy anymore and I thought you wanted a puppy."

The boy interlocked his fingers and there was a long pause. Finally, he spoke, sounding unsure of what to say. "He's just-" the boy sighed in frustration as he tried to think of the right word, "unique, I guess."

The adult let the conversation drop and looked down at the dog as he walked awkwardly toward her, having not stretched his legs in a long while. He came right up to her and carefully sniffed her shoe, wagging slightly. She smiled at him and his tail wagged more expressively than before. She accepted him, too!

The employee gave the leash to the female human and they started moving down the aisles of cages. Dogs turned excited circles as they passed, eager to see someone they did not recognize and the dog gave them all quick, warning glances. These were his humans now and he did not want any other dog taking possession of them.

They reached a door that the dog had never seen before and walked through it into a much smaller room with a desk at the front. Behind the desk sat another female human wearing glasses and reading a piece of paper. She looked up and smiled as they drew nearer.

"I see someone's going home today," she said, looking down at the dog over her glasses. Then she turned to his new owners, "I'm so glad you chose him- he's been here for quite awhile. I don't know what his history is but he might have some behavioral problems, so just take things slow with him." The boy and other female both nodded and the human behind the desk continued, "Well, that's that. Now, just sign here-"she gave the boy a piece of paper and a pen. The boy finished signing and then handed the paper to his mother, who also signed. She handed it back to the female behind the desk. "We'll keep this on file and you can call us if you have any problems."

She smiled at them as they turned to leave. The dog took one last, fleeting look at his surroundings before stepping out into the unknown.

Chapter 2

A New Home

As the trio stepped outside into the sunlight, the dog was momentarily blinded by the brightness of the new scene. He blinked for awhile and shook his head until he became used to the sun.

They walked along a sidewalk for awhile, around the building. The dog had gone this route before on short walks with employees. Soon, though, they reached an area he had never been to before. He was nervous to enter unfamiliar territory and hesitated before he followed his owners.

The boy saw that he was uneasy and put his hand on the dog's head. He rubbed it slightly. "We're gonna take you home, buddy." The rubbing felt good and as the human took his hand away, the dog found himself wishing for it back on his head. They started moving and, as the dog lifted his eyes to see where it was they were going, he pulled back in surprise.

He had never seen anything like this before! Just a few feet off and resting on one long strip of rough cement were rows and rows of odd, shining contraptions. The sun glinted off their metal coatings and hurt his eyes. He growled at them but they did nothing. He became somewhat afraid as they came closer and closer to these huge monsters. He glanced at the boy and sensed no trace of uncertainty in his step which made him feel calmer.

As they reached a particular metal monster and stopped, the dog began sniffing it thoroughly. It did not smell dangerous or even alive and so, as one of the humans opened a door, he jumped inside without hesitation. As the boy climbed in next to him and shut the door, the dog looked around.

It was not dark or scary like he had imagined. In fact, it was rather pleasing. He was sitting on some kind of seat. The material felt strange under his paws, similar to a blanket. He was just getting situated when a loud noise startled him. He looked around quickly, trying to find the source of the rumbling. Where was it coming from?

He felt the seat under him give a jerk and a strange sensation spread over him- they were moving! He turned an agitated circle on the seat and then sat down again, panting. The boy rested his hand on the dog's back, "Calm down, boy, it's okay."

Again, the dog looked to his owner for reassurance. The boy did not seem frightened. He regained his composure and laid his head on the human's lap.

They moved on in silence for awhile until a voice startled him.

"So… have you thought of a name yet, Craig?" It was the mother. The dog hadn't noticed her. She was sitting in another seat closer to the front of the monster.

"I think so," he scratched his chin.

"What is it?"

"Fritzy."

The female smiled, "I like that name."

The boy nodded and looked at the dog, "Fritzy it is."

"The dog" became "Fritzy" and "the boy" became

"Craig". Fritzy was surprised at how quickly he managed to pick up on this. He noticed the way that either of the humans always looked at him before saying the word and so concluded it must be his new name. Fritzy. He liked the sound of it and it was easy to hear when the humans said it. He was excited, as he had never been given a name before.

• • •

They continued their cruise and gradually, Fritzy gathered enough confidence to stand up and look out the small windows at the blurred scenery. It was strange to be moving at this speed without using any effort. He was about to turn around and see what the view was like through the other window when they suddenly began to slow.

They pulled up in front of a very small building that Fritzy recognized immediately as a house. He had listened to other dogs' descriptions of them enough to realize what a house looked like and that the humans lived in them. He wanted to see what everything smelled like and was eager to get out of this metal monster. Here he was at his new home, and the start of a new and hopefully happier life.

He jumped out of the metal thing and started running toward a bush, wanting to sniff it. He got about halfway there and then was stopped short as something tugged at him from around his neck. He had completely forgotten about the leash. Craig held it firmly in one hand.

"Fritzy, come!" Fritzy looked up at the boy for a brief second. The firm tone was confusing and he could not understand what the boy wanted. He ignored Craig and started sniffing the ground. Suddenly, there was an explosion of barking as a dog came bounding toward Fritzy out of nowhere.

The dog was small and had a white coat with brown splotches. He approached Fritzy much too quickly, without any warning. Fritzy had never been more than two feet away from any dog and was shocked by how close the other got. Without thinking, he growled and snapped at the little dog.

Behind him, he heard Craig say, "Fritzy!" He recognized authority in the boy's voice and realized that he had done something wrong. He turned to the other dog, who looked taken aback as well as angry.

"Hey, what's the big idea?" The small dog complained.

"Sorry," Fritzy murmured, his mood softening slightly, "I just wasn't thinking,"

"Well you should be sorry! Here all I was trying to do was catch your scent and you go flashing your teeth like that!" Fritzy did not like the tone this dog was using and he was just about to let him know that when a voice called,

"Ralphie! Ralphie get back here!" A female human was standing in the doorway of a house across the street. She called again and the dog standing next to Fritzy gave him one last, reproachful look before running over to her. She picked him up and waved at Craig

"Hi Mrs. Robertson," Craig said.

"Hi Craig. How are you?"

"Fine."

"Is this your new dog?" The lady was now walking across her front lawn to get a better look.

"Yep. We just adopted him this morning," said Craig, smiling.

Craig's mother walked up behind them, "Hello, Mrs. Robertson. Craig, come inside, we need to get Fritzy situated." Craig turned around and followed his mother through the door of the house. Fritzy was right behind them, glancing once over his shoulder to see if he could spot the little dog again.

They walked inside and Fritzy could not contain his curiosity. As soon as the leash was off, he darted over to the first thing he saw and sniffed it vigorously, trying to memorize the scent of everything around him.

The house itself was not very big compared to the building that Fritzy was used to, but there was such a thicker diversity of smells. He could not go anywhere here without finding a new object to sniff. He began walking through the whole house simply picking up scents. Craig followed him, apparently eager to see what his reactions to things were.

After a few hours of exploring, Fritzy became familiar with nearly all the rooms in the house. One room smelled very strongly of Craig and another smelled strongly of the female and another human. His favorite room was one that had a slick floor and smelled of food. He was standing in this particular room, in fact, when the front door opened and a tall male human stepped into the house.

"I'm home," he called.

Fritzy had never seen this human before and so he started barking frantically, warning his new owners of another presence. He was too afraid of this individual's size to come any closer and so simply stayed where he was and continued to bark.

The male human heard the barking and smiled. "It looks like we have a new addition to the family."

He walked around for a moment before he spotted Fritzy standing there. "Hello, fella," he said in a light voice, extending a hand for Fritzy to sniff. As he did so, Fritzy recognized the man's scent from one of the rooms upstairs. This calmed him down. So, he was not a stranger after all.

Craig came running into the room as he heard the other human's voice. The male started petting Fritzy gently. "So, you got a shepherd, eh? I thought you were more interested in a small dog."

"Yeah," Craig admitted, shrugging, "I was, but then I saw him." The male held Fritzy's chin in his hands,

"Look at those eyes," he remarked, "They're

yellow." Craig nodded.

"I know. I've never seen a dog with yellow eyes, Dad. Have you?" It occurred to Fritzy suddenly that the male must be Craig's father.

"No. Did you name him yet?"

"Yep. His name's Fritzy,"

"That's a very good name." Craig's father smiled.

"I know, Mom said that, too." Craig looked proud of himself.

Just then, the female walked into the room. "So, I see you've met Fritzy."

"I sure have," replied the male, then his tone changed to curiosity, "What kind of dog is he?"

"They don't know," Craig replied, "The man at the adoption center said some kind of mix between a German shepherd and a husky."

"Ah," said Craig's father, "I can definitely see the shepherd in him," there was a slight pause, "But he doesn't really look like a Husky to me, more like…"

"Like what?" Craig, looked intently at Fritzy.

"I don't really know, but he looks different somehow. Maybe it's just his eyes."

Craig shrugged and let the conversation drop. Fritzy could not understand a word that was being said but he heard his name a few times.

When the conversation was finished, he decided to go back to familiarizing himself with his surroundings. He allowed the male to scratch behind his ears a few times before heading off into another room.

Just as he had completely finished with all of his explorations and was ready to lie down and rest, Craig approached him. "C'mon, I want to show you something." He slipped a leash over Fritzy's head and led him through a large, sliding glass door and outside.

This was different from the front of the house, though. It was the back of the house. A large wood veranda extended from the door out onto the lawn and then a few small stairs permitted access to the grass. Beyond that, the yard opened up to a forest which Fritzy immediately felt drawn to. Craig, however, had different ideas. He held Fritzy's leash taut as he tried to pull toward the trees. "Sorry, Fritzy," he said, "You can't go in there, you might get lost."

Fritzy whined but followed the boy as they stepped off the veranda and onto the grass. Craig turned and walked toward something Fritzy hadn't noticed before.

It looked like a very small house with a feeble cloth for a roof. A wood ladder led up to a door and a winding chute led down from one side. The entire "house" was surrounded by bark chips. Fritzy stared at it and tried to figure out what it was.

"That's the play structure," Craig said. "I'm going to play on it. Stay here." The boy took the end of Fritzy's leash and tied it tightly around a tree before walking over to the structure and starting up the ladder. At first, Fritzy tried to pull free from his tether, wanting to see what was in the forest but eventually gave up. He lay down in the grass and watched Craig play.

The boy finished climbing up the ladder and went through the door. It was so small the boy had to duck in order to avoid hitting his head. He sat down at the top of the chute and then slid down it, landing in the bark chips with a soft *thump*.

After a few seconds of watching Craig's pointless antics, Fritzy became bored. He quickly figured out that the length of the leash permitted him with enough slack to walk over to the structure Craig was playing on.

He sniffed it a bit and looked around until he spotted something that caught his attention. Nestled under the little building was a small box full of sand. Fritzy walked over to it and scratched at it experimentally. His timid scrape quickly escalated into vigorous digging. Soon sand was flying in all different directions. Craig saw this and came up next to Fritzy, dragging him away by the scruff. "No!" He said forcefully, "Mom says you're not allowed to do that."

Fritzy turned around to face Craig and in those few, fleeting seconds, their eyes met. Suddenly a feeling of intense protectiveness spread through him. He had never known anything like this before and it scared him slightly. Every instinct in his body screamed at him to attack, to defend something- but defend what? There was a very long moment in which both his mind and his instincts grappled with each other. Finally, his mind won out and he managed to rip his gaze away from the human's.

Craig had noticed nothing of the fierce internal struggle and Fritzy followed him as he untied the leash and headed inside.

As Fritzy lay down on the warm carpet, he wondered what had just happened to him. He had never looked any animal directly in the eye before and it had never occurred to him that something would happen if he did. Why had he felt so defensive? There had been nothing in his possession at the time. He shook his head and decided not to let it bother him. He was finally home after a lifetime of waiting and that was all that mattered.

Chapter 3

Kenneled

A month had passed, and Fritzy's bond with Craig had grown very strong. He was just learning how things worked in his owners' house and he was permitted to walk around as he pleased. He had learned many things during his time here. He knew how to sit, come and lie down on command. He had even acquired a collar, and he had also learned to identify his humans without using smell.

He had noticed, after awhile, that they all had different facial characteristics- just like other animals. He could simply look at them and tell who they were. Another means of identification that he had found difficult to master was in the way that they walked. After staying with them for a few weeks he was able to use this technique fairly well. All he needed to do was listen to their footsteps and he'd know exactly who they were. When they were too far away to see or hear, though, he relied solely on their scent.

He had also learned a few words in their language. For instance, the shiny metal monster he had arrived in was called a "car" and the large path of cement it glided across when they drove was called a “road”. His knowledge in that specific area was still strictly limited and he usually had to listen intently to a conversation for quite awhile before grasping what it was about which, at times, could be terribly confusing.

The most confusing thing about living with humans, though, was the fact that no matter how much he experienced, there were always new things to learn. Even in the house that he had combed over so thoroughly, he would find things he had not noticed before. One example of this came on a quiet, Sunday afternoon:

While walking around the house, looking for something to entertain himself with, Fritzy stumbled across the laundry chute. A dark tunnel that disappeared into nowhere- Fritzy couldn’t help but investigate. He cautiously approached it. As he came close he sat back on his haunches and looked down the tunnel, trying to see what was on the other end. In his fascination, he failed to keep his balance and fell down into the grasping darkness. He yelped frantically as he slipped and slid down the chute. He shot out of the other end and found himself on a hard, cement floor. He had grown quite a lot in the past weeks and was heavier, making his landing hurt. This was not particularly what he had in mind for starting off his morning.

He sat up, groaning and checked himself for injuries. Nothing was hurt and so he decided to look around him.

He was in the basement. His nails clicked against the hard surface he was on as he turned around. His eyes searched the grasping darkness, trying to find an exit. Dim rays of sunlight filtered in through grimy windows, giving the place a bleak feel to it. He had been down here before but only once and he had been with Craig. It seemed much more menacing now. Feeling panicky at the thought of being left unaccompanied, he stood up and started pacing in circles, whining. He could not remember the way out. He was trapped in here!

No sooner had he thought this than he heard a rustling noise coming from the chute above him. He looked up. Suddenly something soft landed right on his nose. He shook it off, but before he even had time to see what it was, he was being showered with soft things. Then as suddenly as it had started, it stopped.

All around him were human clothes. He got up, looking at all the different assortments of apparel. He found a white pair of pants. It smelled of chocolate.

Fritzy was hungry and he could smell food just inches from his nose, in one of the pockets, so he sunk his canines deep into the fabric. He could almost taste food now, but could not reach it quite yet. He pulled *rrrrrip*, and tore a pocket open easily. Fritzy found the candy. He grabbed it and pulled at the wrapper, which opened without much effort. He sunk his jaws into it and started eating, all the while smearing a dark brown stain across the front of the pants.

Suddenly, he heard footsteps coming from a short distance away. He could tell by the hurried rate that it Craig's mother. He glanced down at the shredded pair of pants and realized suddenly what he had done. She was not going to be happy when she found out.

Quickly, he looked around for a place to hide and spotted a dark corner that would conceal him. He was only about halfway there, however, before Craig's mother appeared around a corner, whistling something. She stopped dead when she saw the ruined pants, lying on the floor, ragged and limp like a dead animal. She let out a gasp and bent down to investigate the damage.

Fritzy watched her, motionless as she murmured, "What…?" mentally punishing himself for not looking in that direction for an exit. Maybe he could sneak past her…

He meant to move, but his nails clicked against the floor. The human heard him and whirled around. Despite her sudden anger, she looked quizzical, “How did you-” Her eyes found the laundry chute. She looked at Fritzy, then at the chute and then back again. “I’ll bet that hurt,” she whispered. “You deserve it though, you…” her voice became inaudible as she ran her hand across the stained fabric. She sighed. “These were my favorite pants.” She threw them down and then abruptly turned around.

Fritzy followed her as she marched toward a door. She opened it and Fritzy attempted to slip past her. He was prevented from exiting, however, as the female grabbed him by the collar and pulled him behind her. “Oh, no you don’t,” she said. “I’m going to go get Craig.” She shut the door hastily behind her. Fritzy listened as her footsteps died away. He sat next to the door, thinking that she would come back soon

As it turned out, he was right. After a few minutes he heard her return along with Craig. He could hear them talking as they approached,

“…don’t understand; what do you want to show me?” Craig was saying.

“I want you to see what your dog did.” The door opened and the two walked past Fritzy, shutting the door behind them and cutting off Fritzy’s way of escape. With a slight whimper, he turned around and followed them, tail low.

Craig had always been the one human Fritzy felt closest to in the family. He was the one that generally took care of Fritzy thus he was the one that Fritzy felt compelled to obey. As the boy told him to come, he came quickly.

“Look at what he’s done. You said you were going to take care of him and that means watching him incase he gets into trouble.”

“I’m sorry.” Craig looked at Fritzy and he saw the disappointment in the boy’s face. He was beginning to regret eating that chocolate.

“Don’t say that your sorry, just don’t let it happen

again," said the female. "Now take him outside, he looks like he could use a walk." Craig moved toward the door and Fritzy followed, feeling like a fool.

• • •

That evening, the family was sitting together, talking and eating dinner. Fritzy was lying under the table because Craig usually sneaked him scraps of food. He was just dozing off when he heard his name brought into the conversation.

"Fritzy got himself into trouble today," the female said.

"Oh, he did, eh?" The male's voice replied.

"Yep." There was a pause as Craig's father finished chewing his food.

"What happened?" Fritzy's ears twitched as he figured out what they were talking about. The female recounted the incident to him. When she finished, he was laughing.

"It sounds like you had a fun time cleaning that up," he said sarcastically.

"It had to be my *favorite* pants," she mumbled, "I was going to wear those to Vancouver-"

Fritzy lifted his head as the atmosphere at the table became tense. Craig quickly spoke up: "We're going to Vancouver?" he asked.

"Well, it was *supposed* to be a surprise, but…yes we are," said Craig's father. "Grandma wants us to come and visit her."

"Really?" Fritzy could sense the excitement in the boy's voice. "Can Fritzy come?"
There was a short silence before Craig's mother said, "No."

"Why not?"

"Because, we don't think that trying to keep a big dog like Fritzy at grandma's house is going to work."

"Oh," Craig said. He sounded disappointed.

"Don't worry, though," chimed in the male, "We'll

only be gone for two days and we've already found a decent boarding kennel for him."

Fritzy wasn't sure what the meaning of the conversation was but he knew it concerned him, which was somewhat unsettling. He set his head down on his paws and sighed as the conversation turned to something else.

The next day was different from the ones Fritzy was used to. It had a rushed feel to it, as though things of importance needed to be done, Fritzy just didn't know what. The humans were acting strange, too. They spent the majority of the day putting clothes into large bags and compiling them at the foot of the stairs. Fritzy had a hard time not tripping over them whenever he made his way downstairs.

Just as the sun was at its highest point in the sky, Craig attached a leash to Fritzy's collar and led him out the door. Craig's parents followed, each carrying a bag or two. They got in the car and Fritzy's tail began to wag-they were going somewhere! He had come to enjoy rides in the car and short trips away from home. As Craig sat next to Fritzy, he licked the boy's face. "Calm down," Craig said, laughing. Craig's father got in the front of the car next to Craig's mother and they pulled out of the driveway.

After about an hour in the vehicle, they pulled up at a building. It looked like an old warehouse. It was large and set atop a spacious hill bordered by tall trees. The words ST. RAWSON'S were posted on the front window and a flashing neon sign hung above the building. On it were the same words and a picture of a dog with a halo over its head.

"Okay Craig, you can bring Fritzy inside." Craig took Fritzy's leash and the two hopped out of the car, along with Craig's mother.

They walked across the cement and reached the front doors just as it started to rain. The lobby was dimly lit with a dark, tiled floor and a desk made of wood at the back. There were a few cushioned chairs that lined the walls and some old magazines were hung on a rack in one corner. Fritzy could hear dogs barking in the background, he cocked his head as the barrage of different voices reached his ears.

The man behind the desk was thin and almost all bald except for a little hair that had managed to survive around the side of his head. He also had glasses and a brown moustache that matched the color of his hair. He was sitting there and examining his fingernails. He did not notice them at first but when Craig's mother cleared her throat, he looked up.

"Can I help you?" He had a deep voice that did not exactly match the way he looked.

"Yes," said Craig's mother, "we're here to check our dog in for a few days." As she spoke, the man removed a piece of paper from a filing cabinet and started writing something down on it.

"Last name," he said, the pen in his hand hovering over the paper.

"Holden."

"Ah, yes," the man took off his glasses and smiled politely down at Fritzy. "Fritzy, isn't it?" Craig nodded. "Well, he'll enjoy it here. We let them out for a run every hour or so and we feed them four times a day." The man stood up and moved around his desk so that he was standing in front of it. He held out his hand for the leash.

Reluctantly, Craig gave it to him. The boy bent down on one knee and wrapped his arms around Fritzy's neck for a split second. As he pulled away, Fritzy licked the boy's face. He felt a slight tug around his neck and placidly followed the stranger through a door and down a short hall. Fritzy's footsteps echoed loudly off the bare walls and he felt slightly nervous. He was not sure where he was being taken but he allowed the man to lead him all the same, feeling that he was safe as long as Craig was near. As he glanced behind him, however, a feeling of panic spread over him. The boy was not following them, he was watching Fritzy being led away from the other end of the hall, a distressed look on his face.

The man pushed open another door and suddenly, they were outside. Fritzy whined as the door swung shut behind them and Craig was no longer in sight.

Chapter 4
Secrets Revealed

It was drizzling slightly and the sky was a mellow shade of gray. A row of kennels spread along the rain dusted grass. There were not very many of them and they were large. All the dogs that occupied them seemed well enough; they did not look sick or desperate. Even so Fritzy did not like it out here. He wanted to be back inside with Craig. He tugged at his leash slightly, but the man did not relinquish his grip and Fritzy was forced to follow along.

They approached the kennels and Fritzy looked around. The kennels backed up to a tall, chain-linked fence, behind which was an enclosed field. Beyond that, Fritzy could just scarcely see a dense forest. For a moment, he thought he saw something move behind the trees but, as the man tugged at him again, dismissed it as his imagination.

The man took Fritzy down one aisle of occupied kennels and stopped at an empty one. "Here we are, Fritzy," he said. He unbolted the door and swung it open. Fritzy stepped inside and the man locked it again and walked off.

Fritzy sat down and watched the man's figure recede, thinking of Craig. He could not bring himself to believe that the boy had abandoned him. He would come back. Fritzy knew he would.

Just as the man's outline had disappeared, Fritzy heard a small noise off to his left. He cocked his head in that direction. At first, he saw nothing but then something moved very close to him and he started violently as he saw two bright eyes gleaming in the shadows. He froze, thinking that maybe it was his imagination, but then the eyes blinked and the animal in the darkness shifted. Now Fritzy was sure of what he saw. He backed up slightly and bore his teeth, growling softly. A soft laugh issued from the shadows as a pure white wolf stepped cunningly into the light.

He was large, larger than Fritzy and possessed a pair of deep orange eyes. As he looked at Fritzy over the top of his quivering nose, those eyes seemed to glow against his face like two hot embers.

Fritzy was scared now. He snarled and flattened his ears. The wolf seemed unimpressed and looked at Fritzy intensely, as though examining him. "Who- who are you?" Fritzy growled, fighting to keep his voice calm. The wolf cocked an eyebrow, his black lips curling into a smile.

"My name is Canis," the wolf said, stepping a little closer to Fritzy. As the wolf came near, Fritzy drew back, anxiety rising. As far as he knew, wolves were untrustworthy animals, always looking for innocent victims to attack. Canis saw the look of distrust on Fritzy's face and lifted his chin.

"I am not here to hurt you, if that's what you think," he growled. Fritzy felt slightly calmer. Nevertheless, he eyed Canis through a wall of caution. "I have a very important question to ask you, and I want you to answer me truthfully."

Fritzy cocked his head skeptically, "What is it?"

Canis licked his lips nervously as though thinking of the best way to phrase his question.

After a moment's hesitation, he spoke, "Have you ever felt like you have a purpose to fulfill?" Fritzy pricked his ears, thinking hard. He had always known that there was more to life than an adoption center, of course, now he had Craig. But… even now, there was something pulling at him, like a burning hunger that he could not feed. Becoming a pet had satisfied the hunger but only slightly. He realized suddenly that he had been deliberately avoiding a truth.

Finding a human had only been part of his burning desire. Though the mere thought of the boy sent a tingle of admiration down his spine, there was still something else, a voice in the back of his head whispering to him about what he could become, what else he had to do.

Canis was watching him carefully, frowning in concentration. Fritzy looked up, his answer reflected in his eyes. "You are different," Canis said, his eyes boring into Fritzy's face, shimmering with truth. Despite Fritzy's fear of Canis, he found himself believing the words. "I am in desperate need of your help," the white wolf said. "My brother is not as young as he used to be. He is currently the leader of a pack and, though he does not realize it, they are plotting to overthrow him. They think he's too old to lead and want a younger wolf to take his place. None of them are fit to fill the position and I fear that they will very easily fall into turmoil if a rightful leader is not chosen. At this very moment, he is in grave danger. I implore you to come with me and take over as leader."

Fritzy listened to the wolf's words without really fully comprehending what was being said. When Canis finished speaking, it all came together like one, large puzzle.

"Wait a minute," Fritzy said, "*You*- a wolf- are telling *me*- a dog- that you have a brother that needs my help and you expect me to just *follow* you?"

Canis lifted his head and looked at Fritzy gravely, "You are no dog, Fritzy."

A shiver passed down his spine as Canis spoke, "How do you know my name?"

The white wolf snorted, "Do I look like a fool? You think I wasn't watching as that human took you out here?"

Feeling angry, Fritzy took a step closer to the wolf, "What do you mean I'm 'no dog'?"

"I mean what I said," Canis answered, "You are not a dog. You're a wolf."

Fritzy almost laughed out loud. "Yeah, I just ate a deer this morning," he said, his voice heavy with sarcasm. "I have owners and I live a *civilized* life, unlike you. I *am* a dog."

"On the outside, maybe," Canis said coolly, ignoring Fritzy's remark, "But on the inside, the blood of a wolf runs as freely through your veins as water runs through a stream. I could smell it in you immediately."

Fritzy growled quietly, "How do you know you're not mistaken?"

"I thought I was, at first but then I got a good look at you. You do not only posses wolfishness in your blood but also in your appearance. Take your paws for example: the front ones are larger than the back. Have you ever seen another dog with paws like that?" Fritzy glanced at his own paws and then at Canis's, they were almost exactly the same size. Canis's front paws were larger than his back paws as well.

When Fritzy did not reply, Canis continued, "And your eyes. Those are not a dog's eyes; those are the eyes of a wolf."

Fritzy wanted to say something but could think of nothing. Canis scrutinized Fritzy thoroughly, he looked over Fritzy's face and their eyes met.

Again, Fritzy experienced the sudden, overwhelming urge to defend something. It was ten times stronger then when he had looked at Craig. This time he could not help himself. His hackles rippled to attention and his ears shot forward. With a snarl, he leapt at Canis, teeth gleaming, and collided painfully with the side of his kennel. Canis was laughing smugly as Fritzy picked himself up off the ground and shook his head.

"A true wolf is always quick to defend his rank in a pack." Fritzy raised an eyebrow, confused. The wolf ignored him, however, and gazed over his shoulder as a light breeze ruffled the trees in the forest, Fritzy stiffened as a barrage of scents were carried to them on the wind. He felt his very soul stir as the wind died and the scents faded. Canis turned back around to face Fritzy, "Have you ever felt different from other dogs?" Canis's voice was low, meticulous.

Now that he thought about it, others had always seemed a little less observant and somewhat aloof to him. He recalled watching the female dog disappear behind that door and remembered how quickly the atmosphere had changed after that. Maybe he had been the only one that really cared about the dog's fate. There had also been his brief encounter with the little dog on his first day with the humans…

Canis was watching Fritzy's reaction, "I thought so," he murmured. "I would like to know, now," he continued, "if you are willing to help me save a life."

Fritzy stared at the ground. So was it true? Was he a wolf? A savage, bloodthirsty wild animal? At least it explained why he had always felt separated, somehow from other dogs. His mind refused it, but there was that desire again, an unsettling, almost overwhelming desire to follow Canis. To start a journey.

"What about my owner?" he asked, thinking of Craig.

Canis glanced back at the building in the distance. "Who? The human? They don't care about you, trust me. They pretend to care and just when they have your reliance, they beat you down until you become nothing."

Fritzy growled. It was not true.

"I've seen it happen," Canis added.

Fritzy stared at the wet grass under his paws and frowned. *Craig would never do anything like that,* he thought. But what if he never came back? For the first time, Fritzy thought about the possibility of being separated from the boy. Perhaps he would never see Craig again. Perhaps he was stuck here for the rest of his life.

Did his owner really care for him or was the fact that he had found a new home eclipsing everything that might be wrong with it? There was a definite refusal of these possibilities as Fritzy thought of them. Craig loved him. That was certain.

Then the wind started to blow again and scents from the nearby forest were swept over to him. The plants, the water, the animals. The smells awakened a feeling Fritzy had never experienced before. Suddenly, he made up his mind. Setting his jaw, he raised his head to look at Canis. "I will go."

Canis smiled widely, his lips parting for a moment to reveal pink gums and deadly, white teeth. "Good." Suddenly, Fritzy heard footsteps and spotted a human approaching them and holding a leash. "Perfect timing, too," Canis backed into the shadows again as the human drew nearer. "When I say 'go', I want you to make a run for it. Head for the forest and don't look back, understand?"

Fritzy nodded. Then several things happened at once: the human unlatched the kennel door, saying something about going on a walk, Canis yelled "Go!" and Fritzy bolted out of the partially open door. He sped off down the aisles of kennels and across the grass. He ran around the enclosed play area and into the reaching arms of the trees.

He stopped and looked around confusedly before he spotted Canis loping toward him. The wolf walked straight past him and glanced over his shoulder for a split second. "Follow me," he said and continued on without looking back.

Fritzy was able to keep up easily, he had never felt so free before. The sensation in his paws as they touched the bare earth felt like the most natural thing in the world. He weaved in and out of bushes, around trees and over rocks without any real effort. They moved fast without stopping and Fritzy found he was not tired at all- he enjoyed the exercise.

They walked tirelessly for miles without speaking and finally halted abruptly at a small brook. Canis stopped, nose twitching vigorously. Fritzy raised his head and scented, too. He could faintly make out the traces of other canines. "My brother and his pack are close." Canis said, "We're downwind but the moment you cross this stream, he will be able to catch your scent. You become a threat to his pack so hold your head high and be confident. I'll be right behind you."

Fritzy looked into the flowing water and stared at his distorted reflection. He had a few questions that he wanted answers to before he made the decision to cross the borderline.

"Why can't *you* take over?" Fritzy asked angrily. Canis looked ashamed.

"I don't even think that my own brother would step down for me. Technically, I'm not a member of the pack. I was once but I left; now I'm just a loner. I came back once to see my brother and overheard a group of members conspiring against him. They mean to strip him of his authority, kill him and then take over… honestly, I don't think they meant to go that far if it weren't for one particular wolf…" his voice trailed off and Fritzy saw the look of outrage etched clearly in his face.

"Who is he?"

"I don't know his name but I'm sure you'll know him when you see him."

Fritzy nodded, feeling nervous. He had not asked

all of his questions, though.

"How did you find me? It sounds like you had an entire forest to search for someone- why me?"

Canis cocked his head, "All I can say is, my finding you happened by pure chance. I was simply skirting the edge of the forest, hunting, when I saw you. I sensed immediately that you had great potential and were thus, a likely candidate to solve my problem. There is also something very special about you that became apparent once I caught your scent… I will not tell you. My brother knows the story much better than I."

Fritzy wanted to investigate Canis's comment further but forced himself to put it aside, as he still had one more question left:

"How do you know your brother will accept me if he won't even accept you?"

Canis wagged, "Oh, he will, trust me. The most I can say is: he knows a lot about your background, maybe even more than you know yourself."

Fritzy shook his head in confusion. He was beginning to question his judgment in following Canis at all.

Before he could begin to express this doubt aloud, though, Canis was stepping across the stream and into the pack's range of scent. Fritzy followed him uncertainly.

"Straighten up," Canis whispered as they approached a clearing. "And lift your tail higher." Fritzy did so, all the while trying to wrestle two emotions: excitement and fear. "Oh," Canis said suddenly, turning to Fritzy and looking at his collar, "You won't need that." He lunged at Fritzy's throat, opening his mouth and Fritzy struggled as he took hold of the collar. In a few seconds, the strip was lying on the ground and Fritzy's neck was bare. Fritzy gave him a reproachful look and the white wolf shrugged.

They stepped out from the cover of trees and Fritzy saw a large group of wolves gathered in a circle. In the center was a large, smoky gray wolf with a white-tipped tail.

He was lean and muscular with a severe, pointed look to him. His eyes were a flaming, iridescent shade of yellow and added to his sternness all the more. He spoke to the wolves around him with a voice that was light and casual yet full of authority. His commanding appearance left no doubt in Fritzy's mind that this was the leader.

"Let me go first," Canis whispered, stepping in front of Fritzy.

The gray wolf stopped talking as Canis approached. The surrounding wolves all looked around, confused by the sudden interruption. Canis dipped his head slightly to the gray wolf, "Hello, Twilight."

There was a tense pause and then the gray wolf wagged, "Canis? What are you-" he stopped dead as the wind shifted and he caught Fritzy's scent. For a moment, as he turned his head, a look of pure shock crossed his face, but as he saw Fritzy standing off to the side, it faded quickly. Instead, he simply stared at Fritzy with his head cocked at an odd angle and a perplexed look in his eyes.

"Who is this?" he asked Canis. Canis looked back at Fritzy, too.

"As if you don't know," he said.

"You mean he's... one of Raven's-" Twilight could hardly speak.

"Of course he is! Look at his markings- look at his eyes!"

The entire pack was staring at him now.

"He's come to take over, Twilight. Things have been getting much too dangerous lately..." Canis whispered into his brother's ear. Fritzy could scarcely hear what he had said.

"Hmm," Twilight growled. "You're sure he's-"

"Yes," Canis barked, "I'm sure."

Fritzy was getting tired of being left in the dark. He interrupted the secretive conversation with a snarl. "That's enough," He barked, "I want somebody to tell me what's going on- now!"

Twilight and Canis looked startled at his outburst. Twilight turned back to Canis, "He doesn't know?"
Canis rolled his eyes. "No. How could he? He's been living with humans."

Twilight looked from Canis, to Fritzy and then sighed. "Come here." He beckoned Fritzy to follow him.

Fritzy glanced at Canis and saw, out of the corner of his eye, a wolf looking at him. The wolf was coal black with dark eyes. As Fritzy returned his gaze, the wolf bore his teeth. Fritzy stiffened and Twilight turned around. He saw the black wolf and barked, "Ryder! Leave him be!"

The black wolf licked his lips and glanced at Twilight with a look of utter revulsion before looking away. Fritzy had a bad feeling that he was the wolf Canis had mentioned earlier.

They walked for a short while until they reached a small valley with a swift river running through it. A large slab of rock jutted out from the base of a hill and overlooked the scene. It was here that the two sat facing each other.

Twilight heaved a sigh and looked out over the valley before he spoke, "What is your name?"

"Fritzy." Fritzy realized he was whispering. He stared at Twilight intently as the wolf thought.

"I am not sure how to explain this to you," he admitted. "You knew your mother, didn't you?"

Fritzy recalled a faint image of her. He could not really remember what she looked like but he knew she had been a shepherd dog. "Yes," he answered after a moment's hesitation.

Twilight nodded. "Did you know your father?"

"No." Although Fritzy had dim recollections of his mother and littermates, he could not remember his father at all.

"I did," A small smile crossed Twilight's face, "We were very good friends in fact." He looked at Fritzy and wagged, "I could smell his blood in you the moment I caught your scent," he laughed dryly, "At first, I even thought you *were* him. You have your mother's fur, I think, the markings of a dog. Other than that, you look quite a bit like him. You have his eyes."

There were still several things that were unclear to Fritzy. Dreading the answer, Fritzy asked, "Was my father…"

"A wolf?" Twilight finished his question for him, ears twitching, "Yes, and a great leader, too." Fritzy felt his stomach lurch. So he really was part savage.

"He happened upon your mother by chance. Needless to say, they bonded instantly and you were born. He couldn't stay, though and eventually returned to lead our pack. He told me all about you, your brothers and sisters… and your mother," Twilight had an intense, faraway look in his eyes as though he were not just looking out at the valley but into his memories, "He couldn't stop talking about her for months."

"What was his name?"

"Raven."

Fritzy had gathered enough from the way Twilight was talking about Raven to understand that his father was gone. He wasn't completely sure if he wanted to know how but he asked anyway, "What happened to him?"

At first, Fritzy thought that Twilight had not heard him; he was staring at the valley below them with a look of both mild sorrow and absorption. For a moment, Fritzy was reminded of Canis, the two had the same way of appearing mysterious and extremely intelligent. Fritzy opened his mouth to repeat the question when Twilight finally answered him. "There is something you should know: in a wolf pack, any wolf who thinks he has the right to lead can challenge the current leader or 'Alpha'. The challenge is a fight during which the victor often must kill the loser. The winner is automatically the new Alpha. Raven got caught in one of those fights, challenged for his rank by Ryder…he didn't win."

Fritzy tried to recover quickly from the shock of Twilight's story; he had not expected his father to have died in a fight. He had thought that perhaps the wolf had simply left the pack. His throat constricted somewhat. Never knowing his father didn't change the fact of his death.

He opened his mouth to ask another question when Twilight suddenly continued, in a guarded tone. "'Don't worry, old friend, I can take Ryder any day,' That was what he told me before they started fighting. I believed him, too. Raven was a much better fighter than Ryder and it looked like he was winning. Then he slipped." Twilight took a deep breath. "Ryder tore open his throat. It should have killed him instantly but it didn't. No one could do anything and he stayed alive for an entire day before his heart stopped beating." Twilight shivered. "In all my days, I have never seen such a violent ending. A wolf is taught, from birth, to make a clean, painless kill, but Ryder is different somehow. He *chose* to let Raven suffer when he could have ended it quickly. Ryder thought he possessed the 'right' way to lead a pack and I believe that killing Raven was something of a pleasure to him." Fritzy realized his mouth was still hanging open and closed it quickly. Twilight seemed to have regained his composure and as he continued talking his eyes flashed angrily. "I was furious with Ryder for committing such an atrocity. Late one night, I snuck out and challenged him. By morning I was the new Alpha, and have been for a long time now."

Fritzy suddenly felt a burning hatred toward Ryder, "Why is he still alive?" Fritzy winced as he had asked this with more malice than he had intended. Twilight hung his head.

"I am a coward, Fritzy," he mumbled. "I could not kill him- I have never killed another wolf. Even now, as he sits, plotting to kill *me*- and I'm sure that's what he's doing because I can see it in his eyes- I don't think I could kill him. I could never kill anyone." Twilight lifted his head and suddenly, his tone changed, "But that's why you are here, isn't it?" Fritzy was caught off guard and he wasn't sure how to respond. Suddenly, the aspect of leading a pack sounded much more perilous than it had earlier. "Are you willing to set aside uncertainty and follow the Law?" Twilight continued, cocking his head.

"The Law?"

"Simple guidelines set down for all wild wolves. Only a few rules need to be taught but most come purely from instinct. The Law shapes our lives and allows us to maintain an orderly pack." Fritzy opened his mouth to tell Twilight that he didn't know the Law but Twilight was one step ahead of him.

"There are six basic parts of the Law that you need to know before you become Alpha and they are these:

"A wolf pack consists of at least three members, one Alpha- male, female or both together, a Beta and an Omega. The Betas are second in command and they can tell members what to do so long as they themselves remain submissive towards the Alpha. Omega is the lowest possible rank a wolf can have in a pack. As a result, they are a prime target for abuse."

"Why?" Fritzy cut in. Twilight's face became very serious.

"Imagine being one of the lowliest wolves in a pack. You would not be able to tell anybody what to do or get back at them for something they did to you. Now, pretend there was a wolf one rank lower than you- the only one you could vent your anger on without getting chastised for it. Does that make sense?"

Fritzy nodded. It did make sense but it also seemed cruel and cold to him. "Is Ryder the Omega?"

Twilight looked angry. "No. He is one rank above Omega. If I had power over how the pack is ranked, he would be, unfortunately, that is for the others to work out.

Most of the time, a wolf will gradually conform to a certain rank due to their nature." When Fritzy did not speak, Twilight continued, "Now… as I was saying, a wolf has the right to challenge an Alpha for his or her rank. A wolf must always respect another pack's territory and never cross the borderline without permission. An Omega cannot discipline other pack members- that privilege is reserved for higher ranked members. A wolf is not allowed to mate with others in their pack until he or she is at least two years of age, they can also disperse from their pack at this age to go in search of a new one or start their own."

Twilight had reeled these off so fast, it made Fritzy feel dizzy. When he asked, "Can you remember these?" Fritzy only nodded. He should not have followed Canis. Here he was, about to become the leader of a pack of bloodthirsty wolves. He shuddered as Twilight stood up and started speaking again.

"It's getting dark, the pack will be restless. Are you ready to become Alpha?"

"Yes," Fritzy said, in truth he did not feel ready… or willing.

"Then I give you permission to lead this pack," Twilight dipped his head and lowered his tail.

"That's it?"

"Were you expecting more?"

Fritzy did not reply. It had felt so subtle but he realized that Twilight's entire disposition had shifted slightly. He now regarded Fritzy with his tail and head lowered a fraction. Suddenly, though, Twilight stiffened and they made direct eye contact. Instantly, Fritzy jumped on him and pinned him flat on his back with his throat exposed. Growling, he let Twilight get up.

"Why do I do that?" Fritzy asked, panting.

Twilight laughed. "It is a perfectly normal reaction for a dominant wolf. When another makes eye contact with you, it is a challenge of authority. Only wolves with the natural makings of an Alpha are able to enforce their power promptly enough to avoid a threat. You should be fine. The first few days will be difficult but after they see that you won't give in, they will accept you as Alpha."

• • •

Fritzy felt a building sense of dread as he and Twilight approached the clearing. Then, remembering Canis's advice cleared his mind of any doubt and raised his head. They walked past the leaves and were in full view of the pack. All eyes were on Fritzy as they moved farther into the open. Ryder looked livid; he glared at Fritzy with utter contempt. The wolves all sensed that Fritzy held power over them. Most flattened their ears and crouched in submission, looking satisfied with the change in power. Ryder, however, stiffened defiantly. Fritzy looked at him, daring him to make direct eye contact. Those dark eyes searched his face, looking for a weakness or the slightest sign of uncertainty and their gazes locked. Fritzy felt his hackles ripple and he growled a warning. When Ryder did not submit, Fritzy sprang. In one, swift flash of teeth, Fritzy had created a deep scratch down Ryder's muzzle. The black wolf yelped and backed away hastily with his tail tucked.

Fritzy looked around triumphantly as Ryder's tail disappeared into the trees. He spotted Canis, who smiled. The white wolf winked surreptitiously, turned and left.

Chapter 5

Angela

The next two days were just as Twilight had predicted, it was hard to keep the pack in order. Fritzy found that a swift nip on the muzzle was enough to subdue any disputes. The problem was, every time he got one wolf to submit, another was always challenging him. Fights broke out constantly over the simplest things. Stolen bones and wrong posture were the primary causes of the scuffles. Even in play there would often be clashing of teeth and vicious snarls.

By the third day, however, things had smoothed out. When he told a member to do something, they would do it obediently. Generally, the whole pack was very good at bending to his will; Ryder was the only one that seemed unable to accept the fact that he was now Alpha.

Every time Fritzy came close to him, Ryder was ready with a snarl. Fritzy had learned to be constantly vigilant, as Ryder often leapt out at him when he least expected it. Fritzy became very good at predicting when the wolf was about to attack. Still, he did not like Ryder- nor did he care for any of the others- and found it best to avoid them all.

On the fourth night of his stay with the wolves, he sat near a pond and stared at the reflection of the stars. He had begun to realize just how brutal life with them could be. To him, they seemed cold and ruthless. He glared at the rippling water. Was he really one of them? His reflection stared back at him with deep yellow eyes. A wolf's eyes. Angrily, he splashed his paw into the water, breaking the surface and shattering his image.

He was about to walk away when a voice behind him made him jump. "We are not like you think we are." Fritzy whipped around to see who had spoken.

Standing behind him was a gorgeous female wolf. The moonlight that sifted through the trees seemed drawn to her, it cast a faint glow as it glinted off her fur. She was the stereotypical gray and white colors of the wolf but her eyes were a stunning golden orange, like the leaves on a chilly, autumn day. She had to be the most beautiful thing he had ever seen and he was momentarily stunned beyond words by her sudden appearance.

"I- what?" He stuttered.

She arched an eyebrow, "You think wolves are just cruel, wild animals."

Fritzy blinked. He looked at her directly and had a hard time gathering his thoughts. Hastily, he looked back at the water. "And how do you know that?"

She sniffed coldly, "Do you think I haven't noticed the way you look at us? I can see it in your face whenever you talk to Twilight."

Fritzy didn't know how to respond, he simply stared at her.

"We're not just a pack of heartless monsters."

At this, Fritzy grew angry and found his voice, "Then what do you call Ryder?"

"*Ryder* is different- none of us are like that! Don't judge the entire pack based on one particular wolf! We all have feelings- we all love!" Fritzy did not like her accusatory tone. He growled.

"Oh really? The entire time I've led these wolves, all I've seen is a bunch of vicious snarling canines!"

Her ears shot forward at the insult and she lifted her chin indignantly, "Then you weren't really seeing, were you?" She took a deep breath as she looked out across the water and seemed to become calmer. This time when she spoke, her voice was much more level. "Have you ever tried to look past what your eyes see and look with your heart?"

Fritzy followed her gaze, on the other side of the pond, a young mother wolf sat in the grass surrounded by three small puppies. They fell clumsily over each other in their efforts to reach her. She bent her head and licked them gently, whining softly.

"Maybe *you* are the heartless one," she said.

Fritzy looked back into the water, it was still and his reflection had re-formed. She was right; how could he have been so blind? He shook his head and turned to face the she-wolf but realized she was no longer beside him. He looked around and saw her walking away. Despite his sudden anger toward her, there was something about her that he liked. He couldn't place it but as he saw her walking, he felt his irritation melt away.

"Wait!" he called after her. She stopped and he trotted up to her. "What is your name?" He asked, unable to stop himself.

She smiled. "Angela."

The name sent a thrill down his spine. He shook himself and followed her as they walked around one side of the pond. She did not object to his presence and he watched her carefully out of the corner of his eye. They walked for a few minutes and Fritzy felt like he should say something to fill the silence. "So…is hunting fun?" Angela laughed and Fritzy realized how stupid he had sounded.

"Not really. We don't take animals' lives for fun as some think; we do it to survive."

Fritzy felt like a fool for asking such a question. He looked down at his paws as they walked by the mother wolf and her pups. One of them saw the two and bounded over, nearly tripping over her own paws. She came up to him, wagging and sat down, looking at Fritzy with big, green eyes. Fritzy couldn't help himself, he wagged, too. Again, wondering how he could have misjudged the entire pack. Angela gently picked the puppy up by her scruff and carried her over to her mother.

Fritzy was about to follow her when he heard someone approach him from behind. He swung around and saw Ryder. The wolf had his hackles raised and teeth exposed. This was getting old. Fritzy turned around and headed off in the opposite direction, choosing to ignore Ryder. It was starting to rain and Fritzy figured he owed Twilight an apology for his misconception. He did not want to leave Angela but could think of no other way he could avoid the black wolf. He heard Ryder following him, however. The wolf's harsh voice rang tauntingly in Fritzy's ears, "Aww, so the poor dog wants to run away with his tail between his legs. Looks like he's not much of a wolf after all."

Fritzy was aware that only moments ago, he had felt ashamed of his background but Angela's words had affected him deeply and he spun around to look Ryder full in the face. He had lost his patience with the wolf.

He stiffened and peeled back his lips to display his teeth. Advancing slowly on him, he let a low growl escape him such as he had never issued before. He was surprised to see Ryder suddenly turn and run with his ears slicked back against his head and his tail tucked under his belly. *I'm more wolf than you are.* He thought, as he saw Ryder disappear and then, smiling to himself, went to go find Twilight.

He found the gray wolf lying in a patch of tall grass. "Twilight?" Fritzy said, as he approached him.

Twilight rolled onto his side and rested the back of his

head on the ground, looking at Fritzy upside down. "Hmm?"

Fritzy sat next to Twilight as he straightened up. "I need to apologize to you."

Twilight frowned, "What for?"

Fritzy turned over a small rock with his paw and watched as a few spiders scurried out from under it. "For being ashamed of what I am. I should have been proud but instead I was humiliated. I had always thought that wolves were vicious animals and I was fool enough to believe that, even after I met you. I'm sorry."

Twilight yawned, "Apology accepted." Fritzy was surprised; the wolf did not seem angered or irritated by Fritzy's confession. He was going to say something but Twilight spoke first:

"My stomach just growled at me, I think it's time you took the pack on a hunt."

Fritzy stood up. "I'll go around and tell everybody."

Twilight stood, too. "You don't have to," he said.

Fritzy shook dirt off his fur. "I don't?"

"No, all you need to do is howl. Don't worry," he added as he saw the look of uncertainty on Fritzy's face, "Just howl." Fritzy had never actually howled before. What he had thought was howling was only whimpers compared to what the wolves did. He had heard them howl before; it was a beautiful sound that he doubted he could make. With a sigh, he pointed his nose at the dark sky and opened his mouth.

There was about a second where no noise issued from his mouth and he was sure he couldn't do it. Then, suddenly, he was howling. A feeling of total elation spread over him as the sound flowed from him. It came from his very soul, vibrating up through his throat and escaping out of his mouth. He heard several answering calls and when he stopped and looked down, the whole pack was there, all staring at him attentively.

"Let's go," he said and wagged.

Chapter 6

The Omega

"Haven't you ever hunted before?" Twilight asked him incredulously some twenty minutes later. They were walking along an overgrown forest trail and Fritzy had asked Twilight for instructions.

"No," he answered. "Could you teach me?"

Twilight shrugged, "There isn't really much to 'teach'. All you need to do is find an animal, stalk it and then ambush it. Then you bring it down and kill it. It's as simple as that. It should feel perfectly normal- like howling." Fritzy wasn't sure he believed Twilight, but he nodded.

He glanced over his shoulder. The pack was following along behind him, sniffing trees and looking around offhandedly. He spotted Angela and his heart skipped. She looked up and saw him and he hastily turned back to Twilight.

The wolf stopped suddenly, his ears pricked and his nose quivering frantically. Fritzy almost ran into him. He was about to ask what was wrong when he picked up a scent. It was a doe. The smell made his mouth water. Slowly and deliberately, Twilight crouched and moved silently forward. Fritzy followed his companion's every step. Eventually, they came into a meadow and Twilight stopped dead. He might've been stone except for his eyes, which darted back and forth as he spotted the animal. Fritzy followed his gaze and saw her, too. He stiffened and began to slaver. There she was, grazing silently, completely alone. Fritzy took a careful step forward, his stomach growling. Suddenly, the wind changed and she caught their scent. Her head snapped up and she whipped around before darting off. Fritzy barked involuntarily and exploded out of the growth after her, his pack not but a tail's breadth behind.

They moved as swiftly as wind over the leaves and as Fritzy ran after the animal, he was gripped with a severe hunger that seemed to envelope his mind. He sped up as the wolves gained on the deer, their paws pounding out the simultaneous rhythm of the hunt.

One wolf managed to get close to the deer, and he bit at her ankles, attempting to trip her. The rest of the pack came up around her sides, snapping. They were approaching a fallen tree, while the deer could jump over it, the wolves could not and they would lose her if she wasn't brought down soon. Fritzy growled and sprang at the deer's neck. He just managed to clamp down on it as the deer came crashing to the ground, thrashing and bucking. Teeth exposed, he bit into the doe's throat; instinctively going for the one place he knew would kill the animal quickly.

As the doe stopped moving, Fritzy came away, panting, and headed for Twilight. The gray wolf, however, directed him right back at the carcass. "Get back there," he said roughly. "You are supposed to eat first. You're Alpha." Fritzy walked back to the kill, somewhat dazed after the sudden lust that had so suddenly seized him and even more disoriented at how quickly it had left. He walked back over to the deer and chased off any wolves that were near it. Someone had already opened the skin and the smell made him even hungrier. He barked at a wolf trying to sneak closer and bit into the meat.

It tasted good- better, in fact, than anything he had ever eaten. Kibbles, treats, even human food, were nothing compared to the salty sweet taste of the deer.

He kept eating until he was completely full and then permitted the other pack members to eat He let them squabble amongst themselves while he sat off to the side, looking at the moon. Twilight finished eating and ambled over, looking satisfied. He licked his muzzle, which was red and sat down next to Fritzy.

"I was right, wasn't I?" He said smugly.

"About what?" Fritzy asked.

"I didn't need to teach you a thing. You even killed it without my help."

Fritzy laughed good-naturedly. "I guess I'm more self-reliant than you thought, eh?"

Twilight wagged and then looked up as it started to rain again. "We'd better get back. There are others that stayed behind who will want something to eat, too."

The wolves returned, some carrying pieces of deer in their mouths, others carrying it in their stomachs.

The three small pups Fritzy had seen earlier came bounding up to them excitedly, wagging and begging for food. A few wolves came up, too and accepted pieces of meat from others with grateful whines. Fritzy moved away from the crowd, eager to leave the noise and excitement. He sat down near the river and watched the others eat until everybody was full.

The rain started to fall harder and then it was pouring. In just a few seconds, the ground was completely sodden. Fritzy was about to find Twilight when he was distracted.

He heard a loud rustle, a thump, and a yelp. He looked around quickly and saw who had made the noise. A thin gray wolf was sitting in a patch of berry bushes. He was small, despite the fact that he was obviously around the same age as Fritzy. He had a pair of hazel brown eyes with a slight flaw in the left one, an orange fleck that made him seem rather unusual. Adding to his odd appearance was the fact that one of his ears had a slight tear in it. He looked like he had tripped and there was a patch of soot on his nose.

"Are you okay?" Fritzy asked, concerned.

The wolf stood up, his ears flat against his head and his tail tucked between his legs submissively. "F-fine," he stuttered, "Just wasn't looking w-where I was going is all…"

He ducked his head apologetically as though his statement might somehow be offensive.

Fritzy frowned, "What's your name?"

The wolf looked up at him timidly, "Zeke."

He straightened up slightly and as he did so, Fritzy saw that he had a long scar across his chest. Zeke saw him looking and laughed uneasily. "It's nothing, really. Just a scratch…. Ryder was in a bad mood," he cringed and then quickly tried to recover himself by half smiling.

Fritzy opened his mouth to scratch at a bug on his leg and Zeke flinched terribly. Fritzy stared at him, trying to figure out why he seemed so skittish. Suddenly, something occurred to him. "Are you the Omega?" he asked softly. Zeke looked up at Fritzy with his large brown eyes and nodded. With a twinge of sympathy, Fritzy recalled Twilight's words: *Omega is the lowest possible rank a wolf can have in a pack. As a result, they are a prime target for abuse… the only one you could vent your anger on without getting chastised for it.*

Fritzy remembered that Ryder was only one rank above Zeke. He felt sorry for the wolf. What must it be like to have someone like Ryder constantly attacking him?

"L-look at the clouds," Zeke whimpered suddenly, jerking Fritzy from his contemplation. He had to squint as he looked up because the rain now fell in heavy sheets. The clouds were hard to see in the night sky but that was not the only reason- they were pitch black. Fritzy saw lightning flash on the horizon.

"What do we do?" Fritzy said.

Zeke's fur rippled nervously. "Your guess is as good as mine," he whispered, "I've never seen clouds like that before."

Fritzy realized abruptly that his paws were wet. He looked down to see that the rain was falling too quickly to be absorbed by the grass. Even as he watched, it seemed that the water was getting higher. Hastily, he gazed around to see if there was something that might help. He spotted a rocky cliff not far off and could just barely see something set into the rocks- a cave. It would be a difficult climb but the water was rising alarmingly fast and he did not know how dangerous it would be for the pack.

"Zeke," he said, "go find as many wolves as you can and tell them to meet me over there by those rocks." Zeke looked at the rocks and seemed to crouch lower to the ground.

"I don't know if I-"

Fritzy barked. "Go!" They were losing precious time. There was no telling how much longer it would take before the water rose too high. He needed to find Twilight.

Fritzy sped off in the opposite direction of where Zeke stood and began searching through the trees. He found Twilight quickly. The wolf was sitting under a tree and watching the sky with a worried look on his face. "Twilight, follow me!" He called over the raging wind that had started up.

The two ran as fast as they could, the wind whipping their sleek fur and the pelting rain stinging their eyes. Finally, Fritzy saw the hill looming in front of them. There was a small crowd of wolves at the base, all whining uneasily as the rain pounded on. As they reached them they came to a stop. There were a few hysterical yelps and Fritzy could hear a pup whimpering. "Everybody calm down!" He had to shout over the gale. "Everyone is going to be alright as long as you all don't panic and listen to me." The yelping stopped but most of the wolves still looked terrified. "We need to climb this hill and get inside that cave up there." It had seemed more level from a distance, now as Fritzy looked at the cave he had to bend his neck in order to see it. It was a difficult climb but they could make it. He started climbing first and the rest of the pack followed him. He clawed his way over stone after stone until he reached a spot where it was not as steep. He stood and turned around to see how the others were faring. Normally, the rocks would have been fairly easy to scale but now they were wet and slippery from the merciless rain. Fritzy was surprised that no one had fallen.

Eventually, they all made it to the cave and clambered inside. Shaken, but otherwise unharmed. Only after he was sure that everybody was safe did Fritzy take the time to look around. It was spacious. The pack was able to comfortably stretch out with room to spare. The ceiling of the cave was moderately high and stalactites hung from it, every once in awhile a drop of water running off one and falling to the floor with an echoing *drip*.

Despite the fact that it was dry, it was still bitingly cold and the wolves clustered together to keep warm as the wind outside blew harder and the rain became so thick, no one could see outside. Fritzy watched as two pups tussled with each other, unaware of the dangers outside the cave and simply excited to be somewhere new.

Fritzy walked around. He spotted Zeke lying slightly off to the side and staring at his shadow on the cave wall. Fritzy approached him and sat down. "Thank you for helping me get everybody safe," he said.

Zeke looked rather proud of himself. "I'd never let anything happen to my fellow pack members,"

Fritzy wagged, he had to admire the wolf's dedication despite his low rank. He yawned and suddenly realized how tired he was. He lay down next to Zeke and rested his chin on his paws.

After awhile, the noise and talk died away as the pack settled in. Fritzy listened to the deep breathing of the other wolves that were sleeping, and finally drifted off, too.

• • •

A loud clap of thunder made him jerk awake; he sighed hopelessly and glanced around. He had only been asleep for a few minutes. He shook his head and then realized that Zeke was not next to him anymore. His heart raced as he heard a distressed cry echo off the cave walls,

"Kira! Where's Kira?" He looked up and spotted the mother wolf he had seen with Angela sniffing frantically around the cave. "I can't find her! Help!"

Fritzy fought his way through the tangle of frenzied wolves until he found Twilight.

"What happened?" Again he found he had to yell as the gale outside had increased tenfold. Twilight looked anxious.

"In all the chaos, I think we forgot a pup. She must be outside."

Fritzy cocked his head as he heard another loud rumble of thunder. "Why doesn't anyone go looking for her?" He asked, upset.

"It's too late. If she is out there then she's surely drowned by now." Twilight's voice broke as he said the word drowned and he looked like he wanted to howl. The thought of such a young life ending was obviously more than he could stand. He looked down hastily as Fritzy opened his mouth to say something.

"What-" his words were drowned out as somebody yelled.

"That fool! What does he think he's doing? He's going to get himself killed!" Fritzy looked around confusedly, what was going on?

He approached a wolf who seemed to be staring out of the cave at something. "What's happened?" He yelled.

The wolf did not return Fritzy's gaze. "Zeke," he growled. "went out to search for that lost pup- look!"

Fritzy squinted through the sheets of rain and could just barely make out the form of Zeke clambering down the rocks.

I'd never let anything happen to my fellow pack members. Zeke's words echoed in Fritzy's mind like a ghostly wail. For a moment Fritzy stood frozen, watching the wolf struggle down the slope and then, without thinking, ran out after him.

Fritzy had been wet before. He had been outside on rainy days and swam in a few ponds. He had been sprayed with a hose and given numerous baths but all those experiences paled in comparison to the overwhelming wetness of the rain as it pelted from the sky. It hit him with such force that it stung his skin. He could scarcely see where he was going, let alone where Zeke was. He yelled the wolf's name at the top of his lungs but it was useless. The wind carried his words away the moment they left his mouth.

He slipped on a rock and came down hard on his side. He gasped, trying to catch his breath and to overcome the sudden onslaught of pain his fall had caused. Carefully, he made his way down the rocks. He let out a sigh of relief as he felt his paws touch the grass. The water had risen to almost two feet and Fritzy had to use all the strength he had in order to wade through it.

He looked around desperately for Zeke and spotted him a ways off with something in his mouth. Barking, Fritzy made his way over. A bolt of lightning temporarily illuminated the scene and Fritzy saw Zeke holding a small puppy by the scruff. Talking was useless and as Zeke spotted him, he immediately turned around, heading back to the cave and safety. He walked slowly so Zeke could see him and know where he was going. As Fritzy reached the rocks, he stopped to let Zeke go first. He gave Zeke a grim nod as the wolf passed him. He started scrambling up the hill and Fritzy was right behind him.

They were about halfway up when a deafening rushing sound filled their ears. The pup let out a yelp loud enough for even Fritzy to hear as an enormous torrent of water came careening through the trees. They did nothing to impede the sudden wave; it washed over them and violently ripped them from the ground like mere weeds. It came hurtling toward the three wolves, destroying everything in its path. "Move!" Fritzy yelped as the water swept closer. Zeke started climbing up the rocks, scrabbling desperately.

They were almost to safety. Fritzy could faintly hear the wolves yelling down to him. He wagged in relief as he saw Zeke disappear over a ledge and into the cave. Fritzy made one last leap for safety as the water came rushing up behind him. It caught him in mid air and slammed him into the rocks.

Fritzy felt his paws slip out from under him and he tumbled into the powerful current. The breath had been knocked out of him and he gasped for air only to feel water rush into his lungs. His only thought was to swim upward as the torrent pulled him away and off of the rocks. Which way was up? He kicked out desperately and his head hit something hard. Frantically, he twisted around, desperate to free himself from the water's suffocating grasp.

Coughing and spluttering, he broke from the surface only to be pulled under again.

He couldn't see.

He couldn't breathe.

He was going to die.

He would never know the light of another day, never see Angela again-

The thought of her sent renewed strength coursing through is body. *No!* He thought forcefully and he swam harder, fighting the current with all his strength. Finally, his nose broke the surface and he came up, gasping for air.

The water was sweeping him past the rocks, though, past a branch jutting out from the stones….

Thinking fast, he grabbed onto the branch with his teeth and clamped down as tightly as he could. The water flowed past him, jerking him to the side and slamming him against the rock with a force that made his vision blur.

He did not relinquish his grip until the water had completely gone. As it lost it's force and gradually stopped, forming a gigantic pool, he released his grip and found himself on a ledge. He lay there for a moment, gasping and trembling furiously. He stood, still panting, and bent his neck to look up at the cave above.

It was painful but he managed to make his way up the rocks again and slid to the cave floor with an exhausted sigh. He was instantly crowded by pack members, sniffing him and checking to see if he was alright.

Zeke came up to him and looked him over carefully, wincing when he saw Fritzy's leg. It was badly scratched and bleeding but the pain was bearable now.

"Why did you come after me?" Zeke demanded.

Fritzy shook his head, "I don't know. I just knew that you were in danger and didn't want you to get hurt."

Zeke frowned, "How do think that makes me feel? Look at your leg! If you had let me go, you wouldn't be injured." He obviously blamed himself for the trouble that had befallen his Alpha.

Fritzy yawned, suddenly realizing how tired he was. "What's passed has passed, Zeke," was all Fritzy could think to say.

"Yes, but-" Zeke started. Fritzy gave him a harsh stare and he stopped himself, looking rather frightened.

He glanced past Zeke and saw the little puppy the wolf had rescued, sitting and talking to her littermates. "If I had let you go alone, you wouldn't have been able to find your way back," Fritzy mumbled.

Zeke sneezed. "I think I could have done it," he said, although he looked doubtful.

Suddenly, Fritzy spotted Angela quietly approaching and his heart nearly stopped. Zeke did not notice and continued talking: "And I also…" his voice faded as he saw the expression on Fritzy's face. He turned to see what Fritzy was looking at and saw Angela, too. He gave a smug sniff and cocked an eyebrow at Fritzy but retreated without saying anything, leaving the two of them alone.

Fritzy stood up as she stopped in front of him. "That was really brave," she said. Fritzy felt a sudden jolt of embarrassment; he did not deserve any credit for saving the puppy, Zeke had done that. All he had done was help the wolf to find his way back and had simply gotten caught by the rushing water in the process. There was nothing brave about that.

"Well, I…" Again he found that he was unable to form a proper sentence when he looked her straight in the face. Not wanting to seem submissive but needing a reason to look away, he pretended to see something on the cave floor. As he looked carefully at the dusty rock, he was able to complete his thought, "You know, Zeke was the one that actually saved the pup." He hoped suddenly that the fact wouldn't put her off and was surprised, as he looked up again, to see that she didn't seem to care.

"No," she said smiling, "I meant you going out to help Zeke. I would never have done that. It *was* brave."

Fritzy didn't know what to say so he just nodded.

"You're very caring," she said, "for a dog." Fritzy raised his tail defensively but when he looked at her, he saw she was only teasing. She was smiling, her eyes twinkling. He calmed down, and for the first time since he had been in her presence, felt relaxed enough to laugh. The two looked at each other and time seemed to stop. Suddenly and without warning, she leaned closer to him and gently brushed his face with her muzzle. Then she got up and walked away.

Fritzy stood there, dazed and for a moment was

unable to move. His senses came back to him and he shook his head slightly. He could not stop a smile from parting his lips. He looked around him, grateful that no one had seen that. A feeling had spread over him that he had never experienced before. He felt as though his heart was soaring, and turning circles in his chest. It was wonderful but he simply could not place it. Then he stiffened as a thought came to him. Could it be love? He felt somewhat lost and he didn't know what he should do. Love. It certainly seemed like the right word to describe the emotion. Then another thought hit him: was there a possibility that Angela loved him back? Given what she had just done, he felt sure that she did.

Chapter 7
Realization

Now that the storm was over, the wolves were able to venture outside. The flood had left a river flowing at the bottom of the hill and nobody wanted to cross it yet. It was still far too dangerous to try and descend the rocks; they were still slippery from the rain and after the past night's events, no one wanted to take any chances.

Fritzy sat outside in the sun and looked at all the wreckage the flood had caused. Trees were scattered here and there, some floating in the water others sticking up out of it. Despite this, it was almost peaceful compared to the past night. Everything seemed to be settling down when something completely unexpected happened.

Fritzy was pacing back and forth on the wide ledge in front of the cave mouth. His mind was wandering and he was not paying attention to where he was going. As he took a step back, he slipped in a small puddle of water and fell.

He might have tumbled down off the ledge and

been killed or become seriously injured by falling into the water below had he not managed to catch himself.

Now he was hanging off the ledge with his front paws, his back paws scraping against the rocks under him, trying to find a something he could push himself up with. The fall had scared him and he panted, trying to gather himself together. He hoped someone had seen him go down.

Finally, he heard the sound of paws padding against the rock. Relieved that someone was coming to help him, he looked down at the long drop below. When he looked up, however, his feelings turned to panic.

Ryder was standing right above Fritzy, a triumphant look about his face. He pulled back his lips and smiled. A menacing smirk that sent ripples through Fritzy's fur.

Ryder leaned closer to Fritzy, until their noses were almost touching. Fritzy could feel the wolf's hot, putrid breath stroking his face. "Ever since you first set paw in this territory and became Alpha I planned to kill you. I told myself, *it will be tricky but I can manage it.*"

Ryder spoke casually, as though they were simply having a polite conversation. Meanwhile, Fritzy's back paws scraped uselessly against the slippery rocks as he tried to find some kind of traction.

"I watched you, challenged you a few times to see what your reaction would be and studied your strengths and weaknesses. I know that you would never kill me, otherwise you would have done it a long time ago." He laughed quietly, "Your one great flaw is that you are too soft. You put your trust blindly in others and you become helpless in doing so!"

Ryder glanced down at Fritzy's front paws, slowly and deliberately, he inched his own paw forward and used a claw to gently pry one of Fritzy's loose. Fritzy felt his entire body lurch dangerously as he slipped farther off the ledge. "But none of that matters now," Ryder continued, his voice barely more than a growl. "Because now, after all of my waiting and planning, I am about to get what I want." He lifted his paw and set it on top of Fritzy's. He could feel Ryder's rough, calloused pads as he put his full weight Fritzy's paw. Fritzy growled in pain and felt his grip slacken further. If only he could find a foothold…

Finally, as Ryder was about to see Fritzy off to his doom, Fritzy's paw hit something. A rock! With a snarl, he pushed off of it and sprang up over the ledge, knocking Ryder over in the process. The black wolf gave a startled yelp as he was knocked onto his back. In an instant, Fritzy had him pinned to the ground. He lifted his tail as high as it would go and pricked his ears. He looked at Ryder's exposed throat and opened his mouth. Ryder whimpered as Fritzy's teeth closed around his neck. His heart raced as he tightened his grip.

Fritzy told himself that he needed to end it, to kill the wolf that had caused such a disturbance among the pack. *This wolf killed my father,* he thought, *and tried to kill me*. But even as the anger built in Fritzy's mind, his teeth felt the pulse beating in the black wolf's neck and he knew he couldn't do it. It was wrong and killing was not a good way to solve anything. He couldn't bring himself to take the wolf's life. Snarling, Fritzy released Ryder and stepped back. "GO," he barked fiercely, "LEAVE! GET OUT OF MY TERRITORY AND IF I EVER SEE YOU AGAIN I *WILL* KILL YOU!" That was all the invitation Ryder needed, faster than Fritzy had thought possible he had jumped up and made his way down the rocks, slipping and sliding without slowing down once. He swam through the water and disappeared out of sight.

Fritzy watched the spot where Ryder had disappeared for a long time, breathing heavily. Eventually, however, he calmed down. It was best not to dwell. After all, he would never see the wolf again.

Fritzy shook himself and stretched. It seemed impossible to him that only a few weeks ago he had been with Craig, safe and warm in a house. Craig. He had not thought about the boy the entire time he had been here. With a pang, he realized how much he missed the humans. Suddenly, all the memories flooded back into his mind. The boy had rescued him from a bleak future and an already bleak life, just as Zeke had rescued the pup from a watery death. Fritzy knew he owed the boy his unending loyalty and he told himself that he needed to find him again, not caring how much effort it took. He wagged at the thought of returning home. But how could he leave the wolves? What about Angela? He sat down and looked out at the brilliant sky, thinking hard. After a few minutes, he made a decision:

He would return to the boy.

• • •

By the time the sun had set the next day, the pack was able to leave the cave. They were all relieved to be free of the cramped space the cave had to offer. Fritzy walked among them as they ran; splashing through the puddles the flood had left.

He was walking around slowly, not really sure of where he was going and watching the ground when he saw a familiar female wolf sitting by a rock with her head on her paws. "Angela," he said. She jumped, startled. "I'm sorry," Fritzy said quickly, "I didn't mean to scare you." Angela smiled. She had a beautiful smile. It made her eyes sparkle.

"That's okay," she said. He sat down next to her and an awkward silence followed.

"So…" Fritzy started, trying to think of something to say. It was hard to concentrate when she was this close to him. "What was it like, growing up in a wolf pack?"

Angela stared intently at him.

"Harsh," she said, brow furrowed. "But wonderful at the same time. I grew up in this pack, it's my life. I remember chasing my sister over that rock." She nodded her head toward a small boulder. "It seemed so big then.

We used to hide behind it when we were in trouble. Then we all grew up. My brothers and sisters left the pack and I stayed here. I love it here, I really do but I have always wanted to leave." Fritzy wished he had memories like that. The only thing he remembered from his youth was small cages and barking dogs. Angela must have seen the forlorn look on his face because she asked, "What's wrong?"

Fritzy blinked, "Oh, nothing, I… was just thinking about *my* puppyhood." He told Angela about his mother rejecting him and she listened intently, her ears quivering.

The two talked for a long time, exchanging stories and learning each other's likes and dislikes. They had little in common but even after a short while, Fritzy could tell that Angela felt the same way he did. When she looked at him, Fritzy could read the emotions behind her eyes clearly: she felt as drawn to him as he did to her.

• • •

Morning came and eventually the two stopped talking and went their separate ways. Angela gave him a nudge as a farewell and Fritzy momentarily lost his breath. As he walked away from her, he was covered by the most blissful feeling he had ever experienced. He practically flew down to the river and stopped when he saw his reflection smiling back at him. He looked himself over carefully. There was a piece of grass on his nose. Had she seen that? He shook it off and as he looked back into the water, another reflection appeared.

It was Zeke. Fritzy turned his head to look at the wolf and he smiled. With Ryder gone, Zeke had become more confident and outgoing. He now talked without stuttering and Fritzy had come to realize that he had quite a good sense of humor. In fact, the two had become good friends, despite their differences in rank.

"Admiring yourself, eh?" He said, nudging Fritzy cheerfully. Fritzy laughed. "Hmm…" Zeke teased, "Smiling? Staring off into the sky? *Looking at your reflection?* That could mean only one thing, mate." He smiled widely and cocked his head mockingly, "You are in love."

Fritzy stiffened, "What? I- no…"

"Oh yes you are," Zeke said, wagging, "I saw you two talking. You couldn't take your eyes off of her." Fritzy did not want to admit it but Zeke was right. He did love Angela.

"Aww, you're perfect for one another." Zeke continued, "And you want to know a secret?" Fritzy twitched an ear, humoring his friend by pretending to listen. "She likes you, too." Fritzy rolled his eyes. Of course she did. Zeke stood up to take a drink and Fritzy's mind wandered.

He remembered the promise he had made to himself about leaving. His heart was currently telling him two things- leave and stay. Fritzy knew he couldn't do both. He wanted to be with Zeke, Twilight and most of all, Angela but he had already made up his mind. He sighed, feeling hopeless and he stared at the sky as he wrestled with all the questions that had formed in his mind. When and how? He closed his eyes and thought. He would leave. Soon, and take the others with him. He could not bear to leave without Angela and he felt sure she would come.

Zeke would come, too. Of that Fritzy was certain. The wolf had no other friends and none of the wolves paid any mind to him. Fritzy was the only one who treated him like another wolf and not just an Omega.

Fritzy opened his eyes knowing exactly what he was going to do, the only problem was: Twilight could not come with him. Fritzy wanted the wolf to come but he knew, however much he tried to deny it, that Twilight was simply too old. Perhaps with Ryder gone, however, the wolf would be able to take over as Alpha again. The thought cheered him up but he knew that saying goodbye would be difficult nonetheless.

Fritzy sighed and Zeke looked at him, “You okay?” he asked, concerned.

Fritzy smiled. “Yeah, fine…just thinking.” He did not want to ask Zeke yet. He did not want to ask anybody yet, but decided that it would be best if he waited until the next day. He set his jaw as he watched Zeke walk away.

Tomorrow morning, he was going to leave the pack.

Chapter 8

Saying Goodbye

As the sun came up over the horizon the next morning, Fritzy opened his eyes and yawned. At first, it seemed as though everything was the same as it had been the previous day and then Fritzy remembered his decision.

He took a deep breath as he slowly rose and stretched. He cast about for Angela, deciding to ask her first. He saw her sleeping not far off and he silently walked over to her. She looked so peaceful and he regretted waking her, even so, he nudged her gently.

"Angela," he whispered, "Wake up."

She sat up, yawning, "What is it?"

Fritzy hesitated, hoping that he knew the right way to ask. "You know that I was owned by humans, don't you?" She nodded. Needless to say, the entire pack knew that Fritzy was half dog. There was no real use in asking the question but Fritzy needed to start somewhere. "I've decided that I'm going to return to them and, I… well…was wondering if you would come with me." Angela's ears shot forward in surprise. It was clear that Fritzy had caught her off guard.

"Well…" Fritzy watched her intently as she

thought.

"Do you remember what you said yesterday?" He urged, "You said you had always wanted to leave and now's your chance. Please, Angela, seize it." Angela had an odd look on her face as if she were having a hard time deciding. Finally, after what felt like hours, she looked up at him.

"My siblings have gone, my parents have left. I don't really have anything here, do I?" It was not a question directed at Fritzy; Angela seemed to be asking herself. "I have nothing to lose if I follow you," she added, and then spoke the words that Fritzy had been silently begging to hear. "Alright, I'll come." Her face was determined; it had obviously been a difficult choice for her. Though she seemed somewhat grim, Fritzy smiled. He could not help it- he leaned forward and nuzzled her.

She gave a startled jerk, as surprised at his actions as he was. Fritzy pulled away quickly, somewhat embarrassed, but she smiled reassuringly and he wagged. He told Angela that he wanted to ask Zeke along as well and trotted off to find him. "I'll meet you later," she called after him as he bounded away. She looked around her carefully, as though trying to commit everything to memory, seeming a little more confident in her decision.

Zeke was curled up, asleep on his back. When Fritzy drew near, the wolf opened his eyes and smiled.

"Well look who it is," he said groggily. "Have you come for my sagely advice?" Fritzy shook his head.

"No. I want to ask you something." Zeke scratched his ear and nodded for Fritzy to continue. "I'm leaving," Fritzy said bluntly. "I need to find my human again and I simply can't stay here. Will you come with me?"

"Humans," Zeke mumbled, "don't see why he's so attached." Fritzy stiffened his tail,

"Did you say something?" Zeke jerked upright nervously,

"Er, no." Fritzy nodded irritably, he did not

appreciate the wolf's remark. He had expected Zeke to accept without complaint. His reaction had surprised Fritzy and now he felt angry.

"From my perspective," Fritzy said curtly, "you have two choices. One: you can stay here and remain the Omega or two: you can come with me and Angela and start a new pack."

"A new pack?" Zeke's expression was harmless as he was afraid of angering Fritzy but the sharp edge in his voice was evident, "I thought you wanted to go back to life with humans."

Fritzy sniffed, "I don't intend to *live* with him. Just be near him if I can. I owe that boy my loyalty, at least and I think we should be able to keep a normal pack going so long as we're not too close." His own words disappointed him, as he *had* actually intended to continue living with the humans as before. Now that he thought twice about it, however, it seemed a foolish idea. How else would his friends be able to accompany him? Fritzy was angry with Zeke but he knew he would not be able to abandon his friend. He had obviously not received any kindness before Fritzy had held power, why should it be any different afterward?

"Are you coming or not, Zeke?"

Zeke looked down at the ground uncertainly. He looked around at a few wolves nearby as though waiting for one to tell him not to leave. No one even noticed he was there. "Yeah…okay." Fritzy sighed. The hardest part was still yet to come. Now he must bode farewell to the wolf that had taught him how to live in the wild. The wolf who's life he had saved. Gravely, he got up, Zeke by his side, and began looking for Twilight.

• • •

The gray wolf was sitting near a tree, cleaning his fur. He greeted Fritzy with a wag as the two sat down next to him. "Twilight," Fritzy started. The wolf sensed the sadness in Fritzy's voice and pricked his ears. "I have to leave. I can't stay away from my owner any longer. I know it's hard for you to understand but I have to find him." Twilight looked taken aback and sad but he wagged.

"Dogs always were stubborn," he muttered and then sighed, "If that is what you feel you must do, then I am not stopping you."

Fritzy was glad with the way Twilight was taking the news as he had not wanted to explain things in detail. For a moment, he almost went back on his decision but reminded himself that this was what he needed to do. He felt it in his heart.

"Goodbye," Twilight said as Angela approached them and they stood up to leave. "I will miss you. You were a good Alpha, and, now that Ryder is gone, I am safe to take the position. He was always jealous and he won't be here to stir the wolves up again. Thank you, Fritzy."

Fritzy felt a lump form in his throat as he looked at Twilight, he had not expected this. The two looked at each other for a few more seconds, and an understanding passed between them. Twilight nodded to Fritzy. They would miss each other but what must be must be Fritzy knew that Twilight respected his decision

Slowly, Fritzy turned around and walked away from Twilight, walked away from the whole pack, with Angela and Zeke by his side. He could not bear to look back for he knew Twilight would be watching him with his usual, unwavering gaze.

The clouds were gray and seemed to match the mood. Angela was walking with her head down and her ears folded back against her head. Fritzy was fighting down a long sad howl, and Zeke, though still a little hesitant, was bouncing along, in his usual cheery manner, completely unaware of how much he stood out amongst the two.

They moved steadily through the trees, each of them as different as night and day but all bound together by friendship. This was the beginning of a long journey and Fritzy could already feel the weight of their task pushing on him. No matter, they would not give up and, as long as they stuck together, would make it through.

Fritzy's fur clung to his paws as they stepped through a trickling brook and he stopped as he felt his toe hit something that was not grass. He glanced down and saw a ragged strip of thick fabric beneath his foot.

It was his collar.

Fritzy smiled to himself, raised his head and continued forward.

Part 2

The Journey

Chapter 9

Trapped

Fritzy twitched as a snowflake landed on his whisker and woke abruptly from a peaceful sleep. His head came up sharply as he raked the surrounding night with his deep yellow eyes. It was quiet and only the sound of an owl throwing its rhythmic call into the trees penetrated the stillness. Fritzy let his tongue loll out of his mouth idly as he scented the chill air. He yawned, ending it with an unenthusiastic whine. A cougar screamed in the distance and Fritzy tensed, his nerves vibrating until the shrill note stopped. Giving himself a shake, he turned to the two wolves sleeping nearby.

He did not want to wake them, but he knew that, because it was the peak of the night, it was also the safest time to travel. With a small groan, he padded over to Zeke and nudged him. Zeke twisted around and refused to wake up until Fritzy gave him a nip. "Ouch," he snapped, sitting up. He looked around and yawned.

Zeke's yell had woken Angela. She sat up, blinked a few times and then looked around attentively. She glanced at Fritzy, met his gaze and then quickly looked away. Fritzy shifted awkwardly and then, attempting to recover himself, cleared his throat. He looked carefully into the distance, trying to find some clue as to where the group should go. There was nothing save it be the endless span of mountains, looming before them like a coiled rattlesnake. Fritzy scowled. He desperately wanted to find Craig but he had no idea where the boy was. For now, he was focused solely on finding his way out of the current territory they were in- Twilight's. Fritzy found it much easier to think of the area as Twilight's. After all, he knew almost nothing about it.

Fritzy was thinking hard and the surrounding air was heavy with the silence. Suddenly, Angela spoke, "Where are we heading?" Fritzy looked around at all the possible directions they could choose. "Over those mountains," he decided.

He was in a desperate search for his owner and he did not know which way he should turn. He was lost. Lost! He hated the word. Although he had no idea of which route they should take- for he was utterly unfamiliar with the surrounding woods- his instincts were prompting him to travel in one general direction. It seemed a risky journey but if there was one thing he had learned out here, it was to trust his instincts.

He took a deep breath and started walking toward the mountains. As soon as he began to move, Angela and Zeke fell in one step behind. They travelled close together, for fear of being separated, each wolf stepping directly into the leading one's tracks.

They moved steadily through the trees, stepping fluidly over rocks and branches with their eyes glinting eerily in the wan light the full moon offered. A chill breeze whispered through the leaves and ruffled the wolves' fur, making them shiver. Winter still held the land, Fritzy could tell by the steely bite that came with the breeze. This worried him as it did his companions. Food had been scarce and the bare trees were making it harder for them to travel unseen. Zeke gave a whine as a snowflake drifted from the sky and touched his nose.

"More snow," he murmured, caught somewhere between excitement and concern. Fritzy sniffed the ground as he walked, the frigid air burning his nose. Suddenly, a smell drifted to him on the wind and he stopped. After a second, Angela and Zeke picked it up, too, freezing as well. Fritzy's stomach growled at him as the inviting scent of rabbit filled his nostrils.

Zeke scented hard, "Food."

Fritzy nodded, licking his lips. They had not eaten in quite awhile and, though a rabbit would offer little to sooth their hunger, the wolves still inched closer. The smell was coming from directly ahead in a small clearing. He preceded cautiously and Angela's tail stiffened as the scent became stronger. Closer they came, licking their snouts and straining forward. Together, they rushed into the open with their teeth bared ravenously. Something was wrong, however, and Fritzy abruptly came to a standstill. His tongue hung out of his mouth as his eyes darted from side to side- there was no rabbit.

Fritzy cocked his head, confused. The smell was stronger then ever; the animal should be right in front of them. Head low to the ground, Fritzy stalked forward. He sniffed rigorously as the scent grew ever stronger. Puzzled, the wolves spread out, trying to pinpoint the smell. Fritzy headed toward the middle of the clearing as Zeke and Angela took the sides. Beginning to feel frustrated, he growled quietly.

A flash of wet leaves and something gray shot out of the ground just under Fritzy's foot. With a stomach-turning crunch, the object closed painfully around his paw. Fritzy lurched backward in surprise and agony. There was a terrible moment where time seemed to stop as an unbearable pain shot through Fritzy's left leg. He yelped as he realized that a pair of metal jaws had imbedded themselves into him. A trap.

In a frightened panic, he tried frantically to jerk

himself free, it did no good and the metal bit deeper.

Angela was next to him in a heartbeat, her beautiful eyes beset with terror. “Fritzy! What happened?” Fritzy opened his mouth to answer her but was unable to speak. He gasped and slid to the ground, panting. Risking a glance at his paw, he saw that the fur was bloodstained and it was twisted at an unnatural angle.

Zeke stood off to the left, looking like he might vomit. When he saw Fritzy’s mangled paw he stiffened, gave a whimper, made an odd movement with his tail, and sat down looking the other direction.

The trap was chained securely to the ground and no matter how much Fritzy pulled, he could do nothing to release the pressure. Fritzy’s breath came in short gasps and his tongue dangled limply out of his mouth in an effort to take in more air. Angela barked anxiously and he heard Zeke shift next to him. The wolf growled something angrily that sounded very much like “Humans.” Fritzy tried to turn around and face him but his movements were restricted and he decided not to pay the comment any heed.

For several minutes, the wolves sat powerlessly next to Fritzy and the only sound was the harsh chinking of metal as he tried uselessly to free himself. He began to gnaw at the metal, his teeth clicking against it harmlessly. He tried to pry open the jaws but as soon as his muzzle brushed his paw, there was a fresh surge of pain and he didn’t dare try it again.

Fritzy was beginning to consider giving up and accepting his fate when his teeth found a trigger sticking out of the trap near the ground. With some effort, he pulled at it and eventually moved it downward. As soon as it touched the ground, the trap released its grip. Zeke wagged as Fritzy was finally able to drag his paw out of the trap. He lay there, panting, glad to be free of the thing and yet still in pain. He looked up as Angela whined.

"We need to leave," she said. "It's dangerous

here." Fritzy knew she was right. Though he was free of the trap he was not completely free of peril. The human who had set the trap could come and check it very soon. Fritzy was used to humans but he did not want to take any chances on whether or not this particular one was friendly. Given the trap, he doubted there would be any kind of likability to the person.

Jaw set, Fritzy rose unsteadily. Angela moved toward him but Fritzy growled quickly. "I'm fine," he managed and Angela backed off with a skeptical expression.

As quickly as he could manage it, he started limping off in the first direction he thought of with Angela and Zeke following him. Walking was torture but he kept going until he could push himself no further. Eventually, he tripped and found himself on the ground, unable to get up. Thankful that they had at least put a great amount of distance between them and the trap, Fritzy rested his chin on the cold ground.

It was starting to snow hard now. Fritzy watched a couple of flakes float down and land on his tail. Angela and Zeke both looked around and made sure the place was safe before they too, lay down. Zeke yawned, revealing a long pink tongue and Angela scratched at a flea behind her ear. They were both acting as though nothing was wrong with him and yet Fritzy could spot the worried glances they sent him on the sly. Eventually, all of them curled up and drifted off to sleep. Fritzy had a difficult time nodding off and the pain distorted his dreams.

Chapter 10

A Haunted Dream

Fritzy was back with Twilight and the wolf pack, in a wide valley. Something was different, however. All of the wolves were clustered anxiously around a large black wolf, who was evidently announcing something important to the pack. Some wolves were whispering furtively to each other, shooting the black wolf cunning glances. Others were listening intently. Fritzy glanced around him once and then walked closer to the group. Every step he took seemed to echo loudly as though he were walking in a cave and not on grass. No one noticed him and he stood right next to a wolf having a silent conversation with his neighbor as he squinted for a better look at the black wolf.

His eyes were a rich yellow and he gazed about him majestically. His coat was glossy and seemed to shimmer in the sun. He spoke words that Fritzy was unable to hear, no matter how hard he strained. As Fritzy raked the wolves' faces, he quickly recognized Twilight.

As he opened his mouth to call out, however, his voice stuck in his throat. Twilight did not see him and continued to stare at the black wolf. Fritzy looked around some more and spotted Ryder, standing slightly farther away with his eyes darting back and forth over his pack members, coming to a rest on the speaker. Ryder regarded the black wolf with a glower that Fritzy had received many times.

Suddenly, the black wolf stopped talking and looked at Fritzy intently. Their gazes met and Fritzy saw his own image reflected in those eyes. He became aware of a growing pain in his foot and looked down to find nothing wrong with it. The pain increased, however and Fritzy was pulled out of the scene in a fluttering of eyelids and found himself lying in a patch of snow next to Zeke and Angela.

He shook his head, disoriented.

It had all been a dream.

...

By evening the next day Fritzy realized that the snow had melted and that he could finally put weight on his paw without suffering unbearable pain, so the wolves decided to start travelling again. Fritzy was glad of this. Not only did they need to keep moving, but all of this staying in one place had made him and his friends restless. He watched Zeke, who was loping along next to him. The wolf looked like he was brimming over with energy. He glanced at Fritzy, then grinned and suggested they pick up the pace by starting to run. Fritzy ran too, however, when Zeke and Angela started to sprint, he fell behind, his foot throbbing. He allowed them to travel some distance ahead before calling them back. They returned, panting, their energy spent. Fritzy felt a jealous twinge as Zeke nipped Angela playfully and hastily spoke. "A few more miles and then we should find a place to sleep. It's getting dark."

The moon had, once again, taken its place in the sky as they stopped to drink from a calm river. Frogs croaked loudly from the reeds and a raccoon scampered away as they approached the bank. Fritzy leaned down carefully, trying not to put too much weight on his paw. His tongue rippled the pristine surface and, as he straightened up, he caught his reflection.

He was momentarily unsure of what he was seeing. His appearance had changed drastically since he had left the pack to start his journey. His fur was somewhat longer and had lost some of its sheen. He was leaner and yet more muscular than he remembered. He bore his teeth experimentally and nearly jumped. He looked fierce. His fangs glinted meanly and his yellow eyes looked suddenly menacing. It was a surreal feeling to not be able to recognize his own reflection. Fritzy turned away from the water as Angela finished drinking and locked his eyes on the dark masses on the horizon that were mountains. Perhaps he was mistaken but he rather thought they looked closer.

Zeke shook water off of his muzzle and walked up the bank to stand beside Fritzy. Angela did the same and the trio looked out wordlessly at their destination. Fritzy shook himself and headed down a hill in the direction of the mountains.

The search for a satisfactory place to sleep took longer than Fritzy had intended. They had reached a place where there were no longer many trees, just miles of rolling hills, stretching far beyond their line of vision. The wolves walked for a long time, numb with exhaustion and cold and as they did so, conversed lightly to pass the time.

At one point, Fritzy had the undeniable urge to howl. He lifted his nose to the sky and let the tone flow from him, pouring out his spirit into the wind. His voice seemed to add energy to the barren night and soon Angela and Zeke joined him. Their howls rose out over the hills and died away gently. The short song filled them all with renewed enthusiasm and they started to run. Their calls floated to the sky with more initiative as they increased their speed. When they were almost sprinting, Fritzy looked over at Angela. She looked back at him and in that moment, he changed his tone. His howl rose to a higher pitch and Angela's did, too. Zeke heard this and looked at the two in disbelief, nearly tripping. He stopped immediately and let them run on by themselves.

Fritzy and Angela slowed their pace, still howling, and came to a stop. They sat down next to each other and continued their song, voices interweaving and forming an eerie melody. After a few seconds, they stopped and looked at one another. Their eyes met and this time, neither looked away but continued to hold the other's gaze. Fritzy made a small barking noise and nuzzled her, their shoulders touching. Angela moved a little too quickly and Fritzy gave a start. They both whimpered nervously and the warm display was suddenly over. Angela stood up and yawned and Fritzy looked in the other direction, wagging.

Zeke walked up to them slowly with his head cocked at an odd angle. He seemed a little bemused but Fritzy could tell that he had understood what had happened. He was reasonably surly as they continued their pace but otherwise gave no signs of jealousy.

• • •

For the next few hours, the wolves walked in silence, each lost in their own thoughts. Fritzy was thinking hard about Angela and the recent moment they had shared. He glanced at her and then quickly looked away when their eyes met. Her eyes were stunning, even in the dark. Fritzy shook his head and stared fixedly at the ground, his mind turning to their destination.

When the sky was just beginning to lighten, the wolves found a small cave. Grateful for the shelter, as it had started to snow again, they trouped inside and shook snow off of their fur. Fritzy curled up tightly in one corner and was pleased to see Angela situate herself close to him. Zeke looked at the two blankly and lay down a few feet away.

The morning sun splashed the cave walls with a peaceful shade of yellow, warming their faces. Fritzy fidgeted and then settled down and let sleep cover him like the snow had. Random pictures flashed through his mind as he drifted off and gradually the pictures formed a dream.

The same black wolf that had dominated his previous vision was running through a thick forest. Fritzy caught glimpses of him as he sped through the wood, his tail streaking out behind him like a leaf caught in the breeze. Fritzy ran after him, trying to catch up but was unable to get close. The wolf stopped at a pond, panting, his breath coming in puffs of steam. Fritzy halted a few yards away, sitting motionless by a tree, unsure of whether or not to approach.

The black wolf looked into the water and- even from the distance he was watching from- Fritzy could see his bright yellow eyes. A wolf's eyes. They pierced the water and shimmered on the surface. Then the wolf blinked, disrupting the intensity of his own gaze and swung around. His stunning eyes found Fritzy standing there and an odd expression crossed his face, "Who are you?" He demanded. His voice sounded distant and echoed unnaturally as though his words were uttered by a specter. Fritzy intended to take a step forward but instead he fell, through the ground and then through the sky until he fell into nothing.

He opened his eyes, startled to see light streaming through the cave mouth. The dream had been short and yet he was sure he had been asleep for quite awhile.

He frowned and glanced around. Angela had edged closer to him and now slept with her chin on his back paw. Zeke had rolled onto his side, his legs splayed from under him. Resting his own chin across his legs, Fritzy thought about the dream. It seemed similar to the one he had experienced while at the adoption center. His thoughts turned to the black wolf. Who was he supposed to be? He lifted his head as he abruptly realized something: his eyes. They were the same as Fritzy's. That could mean only one thing- the wolf in his dream had been Raven. "*You have his eyes.*" Twilight had said. Fritzy shivered. It felt strange seeing his father in dreams, having never met him. A bird chirped outside and Fritzy became distracted as he realized how sunny it was. The snow had completely melted and the air had a clean, crisp feel to it. It was pleasantly warm and the sky held few clouds. It was a beautiful day. Being careful not to wake Angela, he moved his foot out from under her chin and stood up. He had turned around and was heading for the cave entrance when he heard Angela shift behind him. He had woken her after all. Fritzy sat down as she approached him and looked out at the sun shining over the wet grass.

Chapter 11
The Lifelong Bond

"So spring has finally started," Angela said as she, too surveyed the scene. Fritzy nodded. It was still wet but he could already sense life beginning to seep into the atmosphere. It filled him with pleasure as he looked down and saw a small group of purple flowers blooming at his feet, their little buds just beginning to perk up. Fritzy felt Angela's eyes on him and looked at her to see that she was watching him from the corner of her eye. Fritzy smiled and wagged his tail. She wagged back.

Fritzy was wondering if he should say or do anything affectionate when Angela suddenly stood. She whined softly and dipped the front part of her body down, inviting him to play. He rose to accept her offer and she whisked around, flicking her tail in his face as she did so.

Before he followed her, he glanced over his shoulder at Zeke who was still dead to the world. Then he ran off after her disappearing form. She slowed to let him catch up and then raced off again.

They ran side by side, nipping and brushing

shoulders. They splashed through a stream and Angela found a stick. She snapped it up and held it tauntingly in front of Fritzy's nose, wagging. Fritzy lunged for it as Angela turned around again. He missed and she barked. Baring his teeth playfully, he grabbed her tail in his mouth. She reached around to nip him but could not quite manage it. In her effort, she dropped the stick and Fritzy picked it up. He looked at her smugly, raising an eyebrow and she laughed, licking him gently on the muzzle.

They had stopped and only now did they both look around. They were not far from the cave as they could both still see it in the distance. A field of tall grass extended before them and the blades reached toward the clouds, waving delicately in a breeze. The sun seemed to give off more warmth here and a flock of birds soared through the blue sky. The grass rustled quietly and for the first time in a long while, the scent of flowers reached them. Angela plunged into the field, barking and laughing. Fritzy frisked after her, his tail a blur. He drew a little too close and they both tripped, rolling onto the ground, still laughing, and yipping like a pair of jovial pups.

A bird trilled as they came to a stop, panting. The grass tickled his nose and he grinned widely. Angela looked at him tenderly and beamed. She smiled so perfectly that it never failed to steal the breath from his lungs. She rested her paw on Fritzy's neck and licked his face. Fritzy nuzzled her soft fur and closed his eyes, for a split second, forgetting everything but the feeling of being close to her. His cares dissolved into nothing as he rested his head on her back, wagging. He had never felt this way before, it was the most peaceful moment he had ever experienced and he wanted it to last forever.

Eventually, however, the two made their way back to the cave. They were both tired but at the same time overflowing with bliss. They brushed against each other as they walked and Fritzy wagged animatedly.

As they approached the cave, Fritzy saw Zeke standing outside waiting for them. When they came near, he bounded up and sniffed noses with Fritzy as a greeting. He made to do the same with Angela but stopped short as Fritzy growled. Zeke hastily backed away, a strange expression about his face. Fritzy watched him carefully as he scowled for a fraction of a second. The wolf shook his head and replaced his look with a more cheerful expression. He wagged slightly, nodding meaningfully. Fritzy knew he had realized it from the scents- that he and Angela were now inseparable and devoted mates.

...

A month went by and the wolves were still travelling. They had become something of a very small pack- Fritzy and Angela were the Alphas and Zeke was the Beta. Fritzy had a feeling that Zeke was satisfied with his new rank, anything had to be more appealing than being an Omega.

The mountains were closer than ever now. As each day passed, Fritzy grew more and more excited, convinced that his owner resided somewhere on the opposite side. After days more of walking, they were finally completely visible. Another few weeks and they would be journeying up through them.

That night the three all curled up in the grass. Fritzy was excited and he could tell that Angela and Zeke were nervous. None of them went to sleep right away. Fritzy lay awake; his mind refusing to let him rest and then finally became too tired to think. He closed his eyes and slept.

The world surrounding him was dark. A wintry breeze ruffled his fur and he turned to see his father sitting not far off, looking at the stars veiling the velvety sky. Raven seemed to be quietly pondering something and a noise off to the side made them both jump.

Fritzy saw Ryder slink into view, his tail high and

his teeth exposed. Fritzy immediately knew the wolf's intent; it was made very clear by his expression. Every muscle in the black wolf's body was keyed for a fight-Fritzy could see the fierce anger burning behind his eyes. They locked on Raven's face and a low, intimidating growl rented the silence. A painful shock of hate pierced Fritzy's heart as Ryder continued to advance.

Raven stared hard at Ryder's gaunt form and when Ryder dared to take another step closer, he rose quickly, stiff as a rock and with an expression just as hard. His lips pulled back slowly to show rows of deadly teeth. The act distorted his face and Fritzy could hardly recognize him. Both of them froze and Fritzy could smell the tension. Then he jumped in surprise as Raven charged at Ryder.

Ryder opened his mouth as Raven came near and the two were on top of each other in seconds. They both reared up on their hind legs at the same moment, front paws locked. Raven managed to get his teeth around Ryder's scruff and with a mighty effort, he pulled his opponent over. Ryder hit the ground hard and Raven lashed at his throat, scarcely missing. Ryder twisted frantically and finally rolled free. They reared up against one another again. Raven jumped and caught Ryder's ear in mid air. Ryder yelped and turned around. He slammed into Raven forcefully, knocking him to the ground.

Raven rolled onto his stomach but Ryder stood over him and forced him onto his back. The black wolf snarled and tried desperately to get free but Ryder had him pinned. Fritzy's fur stood on end as he heard a triumphant laugh.

Fritzy heard a sound off to one side and glanced quickly in the direction of the noise, hardly seeing what was there before he turned back to the terrible scene that was unfolding before his eyes. The rest of the pack had woken and Twilight was standing nearby, frozen in terror. Ryder looked up as the other wolves approached and laughed again. "Our wonderful Alpha," he said, sneering in mock respect, "Here he is." Nobody moved a muscle; Raven lay under Ryder's weight, panting. Time seemed to pause as Ryder spoke again.

"Everyone here knows what the Law states, yes?" The only answer was an eerie wind that passed through the trees. Fritzy wanted to shout something but his voice would not work. He struggled to say something as Ryder's voice rang through the air again, sharp, clear and evil like the hissing of a rattlesnake.

"If I think myself a better leader than this mange- and believe me when I say that I do- I can challenge him. I win and he dies. I lose and he stays Alpha. I have won and now we are about to say goodbye to a member of our pack. Don't worry, though because I know that I will be twice the leader he is. You will not regret the loss, I assure you, so long as you listen to a little common sense.

"You should never have let him take control," Ryder snarled, his teeth still exposed, suddenly caught up in a fury, "Look at all of you! Look at how weak you are! None of you can stand to get your whiskers dirty and so you are constantly governed by a fool like him-" Ryder shifted his weight to his front paws and Raven gasped. "Life teaches one lesson and it is this: only those who have become strong and calloused can truly live," he raked the faces around him, growling in distaste, "You are not living and you never will be if you have an Alpha like this. I will show you how to live and survive the real way and if you follow me, you will never have to bend to the rules of the Law again- we will be free animals and nothing will stand in our way!" A few of the wolves nodded in agreement and Fritzy saw Raven cringe in pain.

There was a frenzy of angry barks as Ryder turned his attention to Raven and Twilight snarled. However, some of the wolves were howling in encouragement, having been persuaded by Ryder's clever speech. Fritzy tossed his head, trying to bark or make some kind of sound but it was as if his own body had turned against him. He could no longer move and suddenly, he could not see.

Sound did not escape him, though and he listened, trembling as Ryder laughed. There was another fit of barking and then Fritzy heard Raven start to say something. He had not even formed the first part of his intended sentence when his voice was cut off. There was a terrible gasping that pierced Fritzy's heart and Twilight howled. The salty smell of blood reached Fritzy's nose and his head spun. The last sound Fritzy heard was his father's ragged struggle for breath and the dream ended abruptly.

Fritzy sat up so suddenly that he lost his balance and fell forward. That horrible scene replayed over and over in his mind's eye until he began to shake. He could still flawlessly hear Ryder's voice.

Panting, he looked over at where Angela was lying asleep and saw her twitch. Behind him, Fritzy heard Zeke yawn. There was a moment's silence then he heard Zeke's voice say "Fritzy what's wrong, are you sick?"

Fritzy nodded and took several deep breaths, trying to slow his heart. Zeke gave Fritzy a look of deep concern; he glanced up at the mountains and opened his mouth. Before he could say anything, Fritzy spoke unsteadily, "We are not going anywhere. Not today." Fritzy felt terrible. The pads of his paws were sweaty and even the slightest movement made him jump fearfully. He could not stop thinking about what he had seen in his dream.

Angela woke and looked at Fritzy. She got up and came over to him, laying her head on his back. Fritzy tried hard not to quiver because he knew she would be able to feel it, even so, he could not stop himself. He wanted to pace and he looked around him repeatedly, panting. Angela positioned herself closer and licked him gently which calmed him down at once. The sudden trauma had spent all of his energy and eventually, he realized just how exhausted he was. Having Angela so close was reassuring and he was able to relax and get back to sleep.

• • •

Fritzy woke the next morning feeling tired and slightly stiff but otherwise perfectly normal. The dream still disturbed him and he felt his hate for Ryder rekindle but he could ignore the thoughts now. He stretched out and shook his head before checking to see where Angela and Zeke were.

Zeke was not far away, still sleeping and twitching slightly. Fritzy watched him for a moment. The wolf had quickly gotten over being jealous of Fritzy and Angela and he still teased on occasion. Despite himself, Fritzy smiled. Zeke was such a spirited wolf; he was almost always laughing or in a playful mood. It took less effort to remain hopeful when Zeke was by his side. Fritzy scratched at the dirt.

Hope and instinct were the only things he was acting on. The drive to return to his owner was much too strong to ignore and yet his desire to stay with his small pack also kept him bound. He was caught between two very different parts of himself: wild and tame. Fritzy sighed, bending his head lower to the ground and smelling the soft earth. It was all so confusing and, though he was already halfway through in reaching his goal, he still wasn't sure on which side he belonged because it did not feel right to choose just one. Angela and Zeke didn't trust humans- it was how they had been raised, and would there be a place for wolves in the human world?

A wave of despondency threatened to overcome him and he was momentarily reminded of the flood he had braved. It was as if his predicaments were threatening to drag him down to where he could no longer think straight. He stared steadily at the ground, his eyes burning as he realized just how big of a mess he was in. What was he going to do if he actually reached the boy? It would be impossible to live in synchronization with wolves and humans if Angela and Zeke did not somehow learn the truth that Fritzy had known for a long time. Humans were not as dangerous as they were depicted by wolves. It was just a strange misunderstanding and Fritzy wished his two companions could experience the kind of consideration he had received from the boy. Without Craig, Fritzy would likely have never learned the truth about his heritage, never have met Angela and never have experienced what a pleasure it was to be a wolf. Fritzy knew that he owed the young human loyalty and he could not bring himself to believe, no matter how hard desperation pulled at him, that he had been abandoned in any way. It was a strange feeling. His mind wanted him to believe it but there seemed to be a miniscule voice that came directly from his heart. Every time the thought crossed his mind, the voice would whisper to him and give him courage and reassurance, telling him not to give up.

Fritzy glanced at the sky; it was a light blue with a few frail clouds. As he returned his gaze back to the ground, he caught a glimpse of Angela. She had gotten up and was walking slowly toward him, a spring in her step. Wagging, she sat down next to him and licked his face. "Do you feel alright?" she asked quietly.

Fritzy was silent for a moment. "Yes," he whispered. He felt fine physically, however, his emotional well-being was completely the opposite.

"Oh," she said, "You looked like you felt ill."

Suddenly, Fritzy could no longer contain his thoughts and he spoke. "Why do you mistrust humans, Angela?" She looked at him, surprised.

"Well, I-" She stopped herself and gazed powerfully at him, her expression serious, "They are dangerous."

Fritzy sniffed. "How would you know?" He asked sharply. She looked like she was going to reply but instead she just shook her head.

"All I know is that we need to keep our pack safe.

That is our responsibility as Alphas." A shadow of a smile crossed her face as she added, "The job will become harder soon."

Fritzy cocked his head, "What? Why?"

Angela positively beamed, "Because soon, I think, we will have a few new members to look out for."

For a split second, Fritzy did not understand what Angela meant and then it hit him like a bolt of lightning.

"You mean…?" he was too excited to finish his sentence.

"Yes. I can already feel them moving."

His first reaction was a sharp intake of breath. It was shocking but he got over it quickly as her words sunk in.

All of his concerns floated away with his laughter as he wagged vigorously. Before he could stop himself, he was howling exultantly, the joy expanding inside of his heart like balloon. They both stood up, smiling and wagging, they ran back and forth and jumped on one another playfully. Fritzy knew he probably looked like a fool but at the present time he did not care; the news was simply too wonderful. Angela was pregnant and Fritzy was going to be a father.

Their harmless tussle woke Zeke, who stared at them, mystified. Fritzy wasted no time in notifying him about Angela's condition. When he heard, the wolf gave a staggered laugh. "That's…great!" He smiled widely at Fritzy and wagged. Then started teasing good naturedly just as Fritzy knew he would.

"Aww, you are going to be a father- that's so *adorable,*" he prattled, snickering.

Fritzy just nodded, staring at the horizon, "I know."

Chapter 12

Foe and Friend

Several weeks had passed and the wolves finally crossed the borderline out of Twilight's territory. They were all relieved to be on land that was owned by no one and talked happily to each other. Fritzy noticed, though, the size of Angela's stomach as she began to slow her pace.

When they made it into the mountains, it became increasingly difficult for her to keep up as they climbed the steep hills. Fritzy often worried about her and the puppies she was carrying so he agreed to change their course. This way, she could seek out a resting place. He still desperately wanted to find his owner but he knew how vitally important it was for Angela to have healthy pups and quickly made her protection his first priority. He walked close to her lest anything might harm her as she searched for a den.

Fritzy had no idea what she was looking for; every form of shelter they found would be thoroughly inspected and then bypassed. He exchanged weary glances with

Zeke as this happened for the tenth time and decided grudgingly that he would just have to endure Angela's repetitive reactions.

Finally, after days of searching, she found a place that suited her needs: a tree stump that had previously played host to another, smaller, animal and its young. The area around it was rocky and harsh but very concealed. The entrance to the den, however, was much too small and Angela dug for hours before she finally managed to widen it to her liking.

While Angela worked on her project, Fritzy decided that, because they would obviously be in the area for a long time raising the pups, he needed to mark borderlines for a new territory. He headed out with Zeke and left Angela to her digging. When they got back, scent marking finished, it was nearly dark and Angela was still toiling.

Fritzy watched her from a distance, whining. She had refused his offers to help and he noticed with a twinge how dead beat she looked. Even after the hole was enlarged, she kept working, her tongue hanging out of her mouth and her expression fixed, she dug straight down and side to side. In the end, she had a den about three feet deep with a large, elevated chamber in which she could easily lie down.

When she finished, she crawled inside and flopped down with a heavy sigh. Fritzy sighed, too, glad that she was finally resting. Every ounce of strength and nourishment she gained now would be divided between her and her litter.

Realizing this, Fritzy and Zeke went hunting for her. They ran tirelessly and were both disappointed when they returned with nothing. Refusing to let Angela suffer, they tried again the next morning and this time, their determination paid off.

Between the two of them, they managed to bring down a small doe. The animal was large enough to settle both of their growling stomachs with a great amount left for Angela. Fritzy picked up as much as he could carry and trotted off in the direction of the den site.

Fritzy loped along, thinking excitedly about what the pups would look like. He made his way up a hill, over which was the den. With a spring in his step, he ascended the slope, Zeke not but a few feet behind. As he reached the crest, and the location came into view however, he froze, sniffing intently. His nostrils flaring, he sifted through the surrounding scents- trees, dirt, water, the pack- and instantly picked out something that did not belong. Realizing what it was, he growled and quickly turned his gaze to the den.

From where he stood, he could easily see the mouth of the den, where Angela lay, the weight of her stomach making it difficult for her to struggle. The reason for her struggle and the cause of Fritzy's sudden halt was a single black wolf crouched next to his mate. He kept advancing on her and she, in turn, would snap dangerously at him.

Fritzy caught the faint sound of the other wolf's raspy laughter as Angela growled angrily. "Come here you." he heard the black wolf say as he edged closer to her, "You look familiar. Let me get a closer look at you…" He lunged at her and she pulled farther back into the den, baring her teeth.

The sight filled Fritzy with a surging and uncontrollable rage. He sprinted down the hill toward the two, snarling as he went. The meat he was carrying dropped to the ground with a plop as he let it go. His ears shot forward as he hit level ground and he heard Zeke's running steps as he darted behind Fritzy, barking irately.

When Fritzy was a few feet away from the hostile stranger, he skidded to a halt, making a cloud of dust rise before his eyes, momentarily covering his face. Fritzy lunged out of the cloud at the wolf before him and his teeth grazed fur. As he pulled back for another strike, he caught a glimpse of the wolf's face and stiffened as he recognized the gaunt features and the dark, menacing eyes.

Banishment had completely destroyed Ryder; the wolf was almost totally unrecognizable. His fur was dull and knotted; his eyes seemed to have taken on a maniacal glint that had definitely not been there before. His skin was so thinly stretched over his already bony frame that he looked like a walking black skeleton, and he had several fresh cuts on his face.

It seemed as though the sound of Raven's dying breath was echoing in the trees surrounding them. Hate rose inside of Fritzy's chest like a fog, eclipsing every thought but one. Ryder- the wolf who had killed his father and attempted to kill him- was now trying to harm his mate. Fritzy bore his teeth, trying to make himself appear as vicious as his reflection in he water had been a long while ago. His fur stood on end and he crouched in preparation.

Then, with his tail streaking out behind him like a banner of courage, he jumped on his enemy. This was it. Fritzy was going to end it and nothing could possibly stop him. Ryder had been given more than enough chances and now he had officially reached the limit. There would be no mercy now, no forgiveness. Both wolves knew immediately that they were fighting to the death.

Ryder snarled as they went rolling, slashing and kicking out at one another in a violent struggle. Fritzy could almost feel Ryder's crazed malice every time he lashed out and he knew that the wolf was desperate to take Fritzy's life just as he had taken Raven's.

They moved away from the den and into a cramped, treeless area under a craggy ledge. The ground was somewhat sandy and dust flew everywhere, making it hard to see. Ryder jumped on Fritzy and grabbed the back of his neck. Fritzy yelped and jerked his head forcefully to break the painful grip. Ryder fell to the ground but sprang back up before Fritzy could get to his throat. They rushed one another and Fritzy threw his paw over Ryder's shoulder, forcing his head down. Both snarled and yelped with their heads bent low to the ground, aiming for each other's face.

His paw slipped off of Ryder's neck and he quickly dodged the black wolf's attack. Barking, he sprang and completely cleared his enemy, landing harshly in the dust. Ryder spun around and they met chest to chest, each having risen onto his hind legs. They grappled with their front paws and lunged with their teeth. Ryder's fangs gashed Fritzy's shoulder and he pulled away, his nose stained red.

Fritzy jerked for Ryder's face, his mouth wide open and found the wolf's muzzle, knocking them both over in the process. Fritzy shook his head violently, and Ryder let out a bloodcurdling cry of agony. Fritzy tripped and his hold broke. They separated and crouched stiffly, ready to attack again. Fritzy was panting hard and, as he allowed the adrenaline to die down, he realized how many excruciating injuries he had sustained.

Ryder took a step forward and they began slowly circling each other. Fritzy didn't blink and kept his unwavering gaze locked on his opponent. Ryder's mouth was bleeding profusely and he spat impatiently into the grass. "C'mon, dog! Is that all you've got?" He laughed dryly but it became a growl of agony as he staggered and nearly lost his balance. Fritzy grunted when his left paw hit a rock. It had not fully healed from the trap and Ryder's fangs had severely injured it, he left red tracks behind him as they continued to circle.

Ryder sprang and Fritzy met him with his fiercely glinting teeth. He rolled over Fritzy's back and came forcefully up against the ledge with a yelp. Fritzy randomly lashed at the black wolf, without seeing where he was aiming. He ended up with Ryder's back leg in his mouth. As Ryder turned to try and bite Fritzy, Fritzy turned with him. They spun in a desperate circle until

Fritzy jerked his head sideways. He heard a bone break and this time, Ryder's yelp was earsplitting. The wolf fell against Fritzy, knocking him over.

Ryder landed on his stomach and scrambled up before Fritzy had time to rise. Dragging his useless leg behind him, he forced Fritzy onto his back and began slashing. Fritzy retaliated just as harshly, warding off most of Ryder's blows. He raised his front legs and pushed against Ryder's chest with all of his strength. The front of Ryder's body was momentarily suspended and then he twisted sideways and rolled onto the ground, coming back quickly for another attack.

Then, out of nowhere, came Zeke. He jumped and landed on Ryder, who let out a furious snarl. Zeke had his teeth buried in the back of Ryder's neck. Though he tried to turn his fangs on Zeke, he couldn't manage it; the wolf was in too stable a position. Zeke's smaller build made it easy for him dart back and forth, effortlessly avoiding Ryder's teeth. They attacked Ryder, who, despite his numerous injuries, was still fighting strongly.

Then, unexpectedly, another wolf joined them and it was not Angela; it was a stranger. The rising dust prevented Fritzy from seeing his face clearly and he could not risk a proper glance. He was unable to tell whose side the strange wolf was on and paid no heed as every ounce of concentration was directed toward Ryder.

Then another unexpected thing happened. As Fritzy lunged for Ryder's throat, the wolf moved away, and Fritzy, spinning around for another attack, was knocked off balance, his head struck a rock and he staggered to his feet, head swimming. He tried valiantly to grab at Ryder but he was much too dazed. Ryder, seeing a chance, sprang for Fritzy's neck. Thankfully, he missed and as he whipped around to face Zeke, his shoulder struck Fritzy across the face and things immediately dissolved into darkness.

Chapter 13

New Members

Fritzy opened his eyes and blinked several times before he realized that he was lying on the ground. He turned his head sharply and saw a sight that made his insides freeze. A dead wolf was lying just feet away from him. With a wave of relief and anger, he realized that it was Ryder. He turned his head the other way and realized that Zeke was nowhere to be found. In a confused panic, he sat up, nearly colliding with something above him as he did so. An indignant bark made him jump and he recognized the stranger wolf who had gotten involved their fight. "What the-?" The wolf had been standing over him and he backed away, growling.

Fritzy scrutinized him carefully. He was tan, and looked very old. His face was covered in scars and one of his ears had a piece missing from it just like Zeke. Fritzy did a double take as he saw the color of the stranger's eyes. They were blue. He looked a third time to make sure his own eyes had not picked out the color incorrectly but he had seen right. The wolf's eyes were indeed blue.

Fritzy took an uncertain step forward, and the wolf quickly crouched. Flattening his ears and lowering his tail, he cautiously advanced, whining politely. He nudged the underside of Fritzy's chin in a submissive manner and lowered his body to the ground with his tail between his legs. It was clear to Fritzy that he would pose no harm to him or his pack and so he refrained from chasing the wolf out of his territory.

There was a very awkward silence between them before the wolf shifted uncomfortably and spoke.

"I am tired," he admitted, "and so I will make my request blunt. If you refuse, so it must be- I will leave quickly- but I want you to think before you answer me," Fritzy nodded, frowning and the wolf took a deep breath, "I want to know if you will let a loner like me join your pack."

Fritzy's first notion was a loud and protective *no* but he thought before he spoke like the wolf had asked and decided that he seemed trustworthy enough. "You may join," he said, hoping that he was not making a mistake. They sniffed noses and the stranger was accepted into the pack. Wagging, the wolf introduced himself,

"My name is Berrin." He spoke with a slight accent that Fritzy had never heard before. It was only scarcely noticeable but Fritzy picked it up quickly, wondering where the wolf was from.

Glad that Berrin seemed subordinate, Fritzy felt comfortable enough to speak. Ryder's body lay not but a few feet off. The wolf's mouth hung open and his tongue draped onto the ground lifelessly. His cold eyes glinted in the fading sunlight and yet, they were empty. Fritzy looked carefully at them as he asked, "How long have I been here?"

Berrin gave a humorless laugh as he too, looked at Ryder, "Not long, really. We finished *him* almost right after you went down."

When Berrin started to explain how he and Zeke had managed to kill Ryder, Fritzy cut him off. He didn't want to know. *He* had wanted to be the one to finish his enemy and the fact the he had failed to do so was infuriating. Berrin sensed Fritzy's mood and quickly changed the subject, "The smaller wolf…ah, Zeke- he went that way," Berrin jerked his head in the direction of the den. "Said he needed to protect someone." At this, Fritzy stood quickly, thinking of Angela and groaning as he put weight on his left paw.

"My mate," he explained, "is pregnant. I had better go see her, too." He knew that the newcomer would follow and so began limping in the direction of the den without the slightest of invitations. Fritzy stared at the ground as he walked, picking out the exact route he and Ryder had taken easily because it was marked with patches of blood.

They reached the den and Fritzy was relieved to see that Angela was perfectly well. She was talking to Zeke and the two had their backs to him. As he approached, he cleared his throat and Zeke spun around.

He looked awful. His ear was bleeding and one eye looked slightly swollen but he smiled heartily when he saw Fritzy. Fritzy found it hard to smile back, his thoughts still on the fight and growled when Zeke came closer to look him over. The wolf persisted, however and Fritzy allowed him to clean some of his wounds before he turned to Angela.

"Are you alright?" was her greeting.

Fritzy nodded, "Yes." He gave her a lick, realizing how drained she looked and informed her of their new member. Berrin sniffed noses with her and introduced himself before hastily backing away. Fritzy wagged approvingly; he liked this wolf already and held no doubt that, with his polite manner, he would make a fine addition to the pack.

The sun was beginning to set and Fritzy had a headache. He trotted a few yards away from the group and lay down with a sigh, thinking about what he had just experienced.

Ryder was dead. Fritzy should have felt relieved but instead, the thought made him frustrated. He remembered all the black wolf had done to him. Killing his father, stirring up Twilight's pack, nearly killing Fritzy himself and finally, pursuing his mate. Fritzy had not been able to take his revenge for these things. His thoughts turned angrily to Zeke and Berrin. Why had they intervened? He could have taken Ryder without any help whatsoever. The clash had been between the two enemies alone.

Fritzy whined, however, as he remembered suddenly that Zeke had had a score to settle with Ryder as well. It was because of Ryder that Zeke had been cruelly harassed to the point of extreme nervousness and he carried a constant reminder of it on his chest. Fritzy shook his head, feeling guilty. His Beta had every right to intervene.

Angela howled quietly and Fritzy put his thoughts on hold as he answered her. Zeke took up the call and Berrin joined in quickly. The music died in Fritzy's throat as he realized what a unique howl the newcomer possessed. It was resonant with feeling. Zeke and Angela purposefully let their voices die so that Berrin's voice continued alone for a few seconds. A shiver ran down Fritzy's spine as the wolf's song came to a close.

Berrin had had no reason to jump into the fight and Fritzy found it difficult not to be upset with him. He decided that, because Berrin was now part of their pack, he would have to be treated fairly. Berrin was submissive and was sure to become the Omega. Fritzy told himself that he would not stand to have a member that was bullied as Zeke had been, especially because they would soon be setting an example for young and innocent minds.

The thought of his unborn pups quickly erased everything on Fritzy's mind and he laughed quietly to himself. His taking in Berrin had been a good idea.

He now had an extra member meaning a slightly

bigger number to go hunting with and a better chance of eating well. Overall, more food meant a better chance of the pups' survival There would also be someone to watch the pups once they were old enough for Angela to leave them.

Fritzy shook himself and then slowly walked back over to the wolves as they made themselves comfortable and tried to get some sleep.

•••

Several days passed and Fritzy returned from a hunt with Zeke and Berrin to find Angela lying inside the den, panting and growling in pain. As Fritzy approached her, to see what was wrong, she warned him away with a vicious snarl. "Angela," he called but she would not answer.

Zeke paced back and forth anxiously and Berrin sat tensely off to the side. They could all sense what was about to happen. Again Fritzy tried to come closer and was just as quickly chased off. He stood a few feet back, listening to his mate whine and glanced anxiously over his shoulder at Zeke.

After quite a while, the first puppy was born. Fritzy smelled the new scent and immediately began barking excitedly. He raced up to the den, trying to see inside and was startled as Angela snarled. He could see her beautiful eyes gleaming out of the darkness, blazing dangerously. She would not stop growling until Fritzy was too far away to see inside and he sat down, whining.

The struggle lasted all day and on into the night. As the last star appeared in the sky, the final pup was brought into the world. Fritzy waited for a while longer just to be sure and then slowly approached the den entrance. He was surprised and disappointed when Angela barked at him.

He padded back to his spot and sat down next to Berrin and Zeke, growling impatiently. "Why can't I see them?" He demanded of no one in particular, "It's done-they are born so why won't she let me in? I'm their father!" Berrin shifted and Zeke stared at the ground.

"Some fathers kill their pups," he said quietly. Fritzy turned to him, appalled and angry at the fact that his mate would think such a thing. "It's only precautionary!" he added hastily as he saw Fritzy's expression, "She's just following her instincts." Fritzy sniffed but he could not argue. After all, instinct was the only way he had managed to survive so far. A cricket chirped as Zeke added, "You also have to remember that she is not sure what to expect, given your background." Fritzy knew he meant the fact that Fritzy was part dog.

Berrin cocked his head, "Huh?" He said, confused. Zeke gave Fritzy a furtive warning glance but Fritzy ignored him. There was no reason for the wolf to be excluded. He was a member and, Fritzy figured, should know about his Alpha.

"My mother," he clarified, "was a dog. I was brought up with humans. We were travelling to find my owner when Angela became pregnant." Berrin said nothing but his expression was strange and Fritzy could not tell what he thought of the concept. They all looked up excitedly as Angela's faint voice called Fritzy into the den. Fritzy stood, feeling suddenly nervous and Zeke gave him an encouraging shove forward. The den was larger than he had thought and as he crawled inside, his heart did a back flip.

There was Angela, looking exhausted but nevertheless wagging. Nestled close to her were six squirming puppies. Fritzy let out an amazed sigh as he saw them and Angela smiled. "Aren't they beautiful?"

Fritzy had never seen anything more so in his entire life. He was filled with pride and he could not help himself, he covered Angela with several slobbery licks, his tail a blur. She laughed weakly, "Calm down. I'm tired enough already." He sat down, still wagging, and leaned in closer to get a better look at their pups.

They were all the same dark shade of brown but Fritzy guessed that would change as they matured. Their eyes were sealed shut and they moved about, whimpering helplessly near Angela's stomach. Fritzy smiled warmly at one as it blindly made its way over to him and came up against his paw.

Angela watched him with a smile that made her eyes light up, even in the stark atmosphere of the den.

"We should name them," she said.

"Alright," Fritzy said, "how about-"

"I didn't mean now," Angela snapped suddenly. Fritzy jumped.

"Oh, okay…" He said quietly. She bobbed her head apologetically.

"I'm tired," she sighed and carefully rested her head on the ground, closing her eyes. Fritzy decided that this was his cue to leave and he slowly backed out of the tunnel, shaking dirt from his fur. Berrin and Zeke were waiting for him.

"Well?" said Berrin, his ears erect. Fritzy smiled.

"There are six, all beautiful and healthy." Zeke bounded up and nudged Fritzy with his muzzle.

"Congratulations!" He beamed and Fritzy wagged, suddenly realizing that he, like Angela, was tired.

No one had gotten any sleep lately and Berrin yawned. "I'm going to go lie down," he said. Fritzy and Zeke followed him as they each chose a spot just a few feet away from the den.

Although Fritzy was tired, he did not get much sleep. He woke up repeatedly, worrying about Angela and the pups. He made several trips into the den to make sure they were unharmed. Every time he checked, the pups were sleeping peacefully against Angela and Angela herself was breathing gently.

The next day, Fritzy came into the den as soon as he heard Angela wake. She greeted him with a wag and a gentle lick on the face. The puppies had already started to nurse and Fritzy watched them move proudly. Angela yawned and then slowly sat up, the litter clustering around her legs for warmth. "So, about naming them..." she looked at Fritzy and cocked an eyebrow. "Did you have any ideas?"

Fritzy looked at her, surprised. "I..." he thought hard but nothing came to mind.

Angela sneezed and then looked down at her brood. "There are two females and four males. They are all strong and so deserve strong names." She gazed out of the tunnel into the sky as she thought. Then, dipping her head, she sought out the puppy that had approached Fritzy earlier. "Daniel," she said gently, licking his fur clean. Fritzy smiled; he liked the name.

She pulled another near her and stared at him closely, her brow furrowed. "McKay," she whispered finally.

A female pup wriggled near and Angela nudged her gently. "This was the last born and the stars were shining brightly in the heavens when her life began. Her name will be Star."

She turned her attention to the rest of the pups; all clustered together near her stomach. "Aspen, Peregrine and Bennett." Precariously, she lay back down and the puppies clambered forward to get to her stomach. Fritzy looked at each of them in turn, saying their names in his head. Daniel, Star, McKay, Peregrine, Bennett and Aspen. These were his pups and through them, he would live on. He gave Angela one last lick before backing out into the sunlight.

Zeke lifted one paw off of the ground uncertainly, straining forward. Fritzy allowed him to go look at the pups, leaving him and Berrin alone.

"They have their names," Fritzy announced proudly, Berrin wagged.

The two stood silently, listening to Zeke and Angela talking and when the gray wolf emerged from the tunnel, Berrin left to meet the new members.

• • •

After two weeks, the pups could see and hear. Fritzy walked into the den one day to see them all move toward him curiously whining and sniffing his paws. Another week and their legs were strong enough for them to be able to tumble around in the den. Yet another week and they were taking their first steps outside, blinking bemusedly as the sun shone down on their little faces and moving carefully through the grass having not yet gotten used to the texture.

Finally, they were old enough for Angela to leave them outside until dark so long as one wolf was closely watching them. One day, while she, Zeke and Berrin went hunting, Fritzy stayed behind with his pups, playing with them.

He flicked his tail once and Daniel jumped on it, yipping. Fritzy moved his tail around and laughed as the little puppy sprang after it. Aspen saw them and headed over to join her brother. "Ouch!" Fritzy yelled as he felt Aspen's new, needle teeth sink into the tip of his tail. He growled a warning at them. Aspen whimpered a quick apology and they started jumping on him again.

Keeping the pack fed was a job. Fritzy was glad food was now so abundant because they were working to feed not only adults but the pups, too. The pack took turns watching over the pups while the others went hunting. They would come home dragging pieces of their kill for whoever was babysitting. The pups would run up to them and lick around the outside of their mouths, whining. The adults would then quickly regurgitate their food for the little ones. This way, the puppies could easily be weaned from their mother's milk although they still tried to suckle every now and then.

• • •

Two months passed and the pups grew old enough

for Angela to relocate them all to a new site a few miles away from the den. It was an open field near a stream and a tall oak tree marked the boundary line for the pups. They played and chased and learned to hunt small animals like mice and voles, using their sense of smell. The boundary line had to be watched carefully, however, as the pups were curious of what lay beyond it and would often try to sneak off. They were consistently asking when they would be able to come with the pack on a hunt. Every time Fritzy left, there would be a chorus of pleas. Eventually, he grew tired of hearing them and allowed them to witness a hunt.

The pack headed out in a straight line with the pups in the middle and Berrin bringing up the rear making sure that no one was left behind. As Fritzy walked, he looked over his shoulder repeatedly in response to the many yelps and yips that were floating towards him from the back of the line.

Aspen started complaining as they reached a large slope and began to make their way upward. "I'm tired," she whined. Berrin gave her a nip, telling her she needed to be quiet. After that, all of the pups chimed in, their voices twisting together, each pup wondering loudly when they would find something. The only one who had not opened his mouth the entire time was Daniel. He tottered along, wagging and silently investigating everything he passed. Fritzy smiled at him as they made eye contact.

The entire pack was much too distracted by the whining pups to realize a deer grazing yards away. Only when the animal bounded off into the trees, did they give chase. Several excited barks sounded from behind Fritzy as he leapt forward, gripped with that familiar zeal. He opened his mouth as they neared the deer and, not caring how dangerous his stunt was, jumped for it, grabbing it around the neck and momentarily swinging in midair. The deer tripped and crashed to the ground, kicking. Fritzy buried his teeth into its throat and the deer gradually ceased its movements.

Bennett barked excitedly and made a dash for the food. Fritzy growled at him and he stopped abruptly, whining. He and Angela were to eat first and then the rest of the pack could have their turn. The wolves backed away as he and Angela started devouring the food.

Finished, Fritzy sat some distance away from his pack members, watching them eat. He licked his muzzle and observed Peregrine and Star tussling over a piece of hide. The pups had grown much larger and in a few months, they would be nearly as big as an adult wolf. Most of their eyes had changed from green to deep amber like their mother and each pup had a distinguishable coat.

Peregrine and Star were black but Star possessed a white streak on her muzzle whereas Peregrine was completely dark. Aspen had markings similar to Fritzy's except that they lacked the prominence his held. Bennett was a pure and flawless white which reminded Fritzy often of Canis and was the only one in his litter with deep yellow eyes exactly like Fritzy's. McKay was reddish brown and had a tail tipped in black. His face and chest were substantially lighter than the rest of his coat.

Fritzy glanced at Daniel, who was being repeatedly chased away from the food by his siblings. He made no protesting moves as they nipped at him and backed away, still wagging, content to wait until they permitted him to eat. Daniel was dark brown with a light face. The colors contrasted sharply along with his golden-orange eyes. He was timid, in fact, more timid than any of his siblings; he barley ever spoke and when he did, his voice would often be no louder than a whisper. Angela worried about him and so did Fritzy. His brothers and sisters often teased him and Fritzy feared that he might someday become an Omega if he did not stand up for himself more.

There was, however, something very special about the pup. For, though he was timid, he constantly wanted to learn and he often bounded up to Fritzy, asking numerous questions. He would usually choose to follow the adult wolves around, leaving his siblings to their games.

As he witnessed his son being chased away from the kill yet again, Fritzy stood and casually walked over. He saw Bennett and Aspen look up uncomfortably at him as he approached. He sat down next to Daniel and wagged.

"Did you get enough to eat?" He asked lightly. Daniel nodded, smiling, his eyes bright. Fritzy noticed, out of the tail of his eye, McKay staring intently at the ground, pretending not to listen. "Are you sure?" He persisted.

"Yes," Daniel said quietly, still smiling, "I'm full."

Turning his attention to the other puppies, Fritzy asked, "How about all of you? How did you eat?" There was a jumbled chorus of "fine"s and "good"s as all of the pups kept their eyes fixed guiltily on the ground. "Glad to hear it." Fritzy smiled and walked back to his spot, shaking his head as he went. He had to admire Daniel's acceptable nature.

Berrin started a howl and Fritzy quickly picked it up. They rallied for a moment before Angela joined in, too. Zeke was lying on his back atop a large rock and, too lazy to rise, simply started upside down. His head hung off of the rock and his legs were pointed skyward. Seeing an open target, Peregrine pounced on him. Zeke gave a startled yelp and rolled over, tumbling to the ground. When he noticed who had ambushed him he laughed and they started wrestling.

Although Zeke was larger than the pups, it was not by much, for he matched their size better than any other member of the pack- even Angela. They often sought him out when they wanted to tussle and he was always willing to do so.

The pups were indeed growing and Fritzy realized suddenly that they were big enough to travel. The thought had struck him suddenly and it brought on a barrage of notions. For the first time in a very long while, Fritzy thought of Craig. He gazed out at the horizon and scowled. They were towards the peak of the mountains and Fritzy realized that he was closer than ever to his owner. Setting his jaw, he promised himself that he would resume the quest as soon as possible. He growled, however, as he thought of what Angela's reaction to his decision would be. Just as the thought occurred to him, he saw her trotting over to him. He needed to inform her and so, as she sat down next to him, he opened his mouth.

"Angela?"

"Yes?"

"The pups have grown."

She raised an eyebrow, "I know."

"They are almost as big as Zeke."

Angela frowned at him, her amber eyes searching his very soul. "What are you getting at?" She inquired apprehensively.

"Well, they can travel now and so I was thinking that it would be a good time to start moving again…." His voice died uncertainly as he noticed her expression.

"You *still* want to find the human? I thought you would have forgotten about him by now." The fur on the back of Fritzy's neck rippled to attention.

"He is not just a human. He gave me a new life! He cares about me and I care about him. Is that such a crime?"

Angela barked heatedly, "Look around you! You are an Alpha, you control a territory which you must protect and lead a pack including six beautiful pups who have a safe place to grow and learn. They cannot handle being torn away from it!"

She glared at him angrily.

"Please," Fritzy said, lowering his voice as Star looked curiously in their direction, "Trust me, Angela."

Her expression softened somewhat and she sighed. She looked mentally strained. "Alright."

As Fritzy wagged, she managed a halfhearted smile. It was clear that she was having a very hard time putting her faith in the matter and he nuzzled her. "Everything will be fine," he whispered, as reassuringly as he could. She seemed to relax slightly. The sun was at its highest point in the sky and Fritzy squinted up at it. This time the next day, they would begin the trek.

Chapter 14

Crossing the Line

The next day was unusually warm and the wolves walked about lazily with their tongues hanging casually out of their mouths. Fritzy had told the pups that they would be leaving soon and they had all gathered together under a tree, whispering excitedly in the soothing shade.

Finally, it was time to head out and Fritzy raised his head to the cloudless sky and howled. Nobody joined in right away and so his first note floated away into silence. The entire pack chimed in as he took a breath and started again, the pups yipping and whining as they were still trying to master the technique of howling. The song stopped and Fritzy shook himself. Angela stood beside him and he gave her a meaningful nod before they began trotting at a brisk pace.

The pups did well and all throughout the day, they kept up a stream of cheerful conversation. Fritzy found how invigorating it was to listen to their young voices.

By the next night, they had traveled over twenty

miles and finally stopped to rest. The talking between the pups had died several hours ago and they now flopped down, weary from the strenuous trip. Fritzy knew that this was only the beginning of several long and tiring days. Angela walked among them, stopping and talking gently to each one in turn. She listened silently to their complaints and, as she turned toward Fritzy, gave him a harsh look.

Morning came much too quickly and Fritzy stretched his stiff limbs as the sun rose. Revived, they all began walking with new vigor. After a few hours, they passed the boundary Fritzy had marked so long ago and began traveling through unknown territory. The sun was setting when Fritzy abruptly halted, growling quietly. This was something he had not anticipated.

He sniffed and picked up scent marks- they were on the border of a strange pack's territory. He took an uncertain step backward and glanced at Angela. "What should we do?" he asked her. She swept the area without blinking.

"Simple, let them know we are here. Maybe they'll let us pass through." She did not look very sure and her comment did nothing to ease the sense of disquiet that was creeping up Fritzy's spine. Even so, he decided that he might as well try.

Raising his head, he let one long howl float out over the trees. It faded into an echoing silence and there was a long pause before several answering voices returned his call.

He glanced around him at the adult wolves in his pack before stepping boldly across the boundary line. They followed him, howling in response to the strangers, as they made their way forward. Fritzy kept up a constant rally with the voices as they grew louder and louder, each pack moving towards the other.

Finally, they came into sight of each other. The other pack was not large, it was made up of only five wolves, however, they managed to seem threatening enough. One male wolf trotted out ahead of the others, his tail high and his teeth slightly visible, growling.

He stopped when he and Fritzy were face to face and they looked into each other's eyes intently. "What do you want?" asked the Alpha Male. His voice was low and displeased. Fritzy straightened and lifted his tail.

"To pass through your territory safely. We mean you no harm and simply wish to continue traveling."

His answer was not good enough. The other wolf growled again, this time he stiffened. Fritzy had been afraid of this. Because the other Alpha was not willing to let them pass, he was now being challenged for the right. Reluctantly, Fritzy bore his teeth and took a cautious step forward. He opened his mouth as the other wolf rushed him.

The brawl between them was nothing compared to Fritzy's fight with Ryder. In fact, they made no physical contact at all. They kept their eyes locked as they charged one another, feinting and seeing who would back down first.

Eventually, Fritzy's opponent dropped his gaze and Fritzy raised his head triumphantly. With an emotionless nod to the Alpha, he led his pack past them and they sped off through the trees.

It was getting dark when they made it out of the strange pack's territory, grateful that they had not been attacked on their way out. Berrin gave a quiet sigh of relief as they crossed the borderline. The area they were in now was utterly deserted and thankfully, was not owned. Looking around, Fritzy realized why the pack's territory had ended where it did.

They stood on one side of a wide canyon. Gingerly, Fritzy peered over the edge and saw, with a jolt that the bottom was quite a long way down. In fact, it was too far down to see in the dark. The walls of the canyon were jagged and rocky. Pieces of sharp rock jutted out at strange angles. There was nothing they could do but move forward and try not to fall. The path they followed was narrow, as a steep hill prevented them from moving to one side. Fritzy gulped as a few loose rocks fell from underneath his paws and bounced down the canyon walls, echoing and causing more rocks to fall. They hit the bottom with a resounding bang. Fritzy looked over his shoulder at the rest of his pack; Angela was right behind him, looking down at the rocks with wide eyes. "Be careful and nobody will fall," he said, attempting reassurance and failing miserably. Fritzy set his gaze to the distance, realizing that the path widened farther ahead, and took a step forward.

They moved together in a straight line, putting one paw directly in front of the other. Their progress was slow as they literally walked the line of death. Fritzy winced every time a rock shifted and he heard Zeke whimpering quietly. Berrin was mumbling to himself and the pups were dead silent.

Fritzy was momentarily weak with relief as the path became more spacious. Eventually, there was enough room for everyone to walk a safe distance away from the edge of the canyon. The night was dark as pitch and the moon glowed eerily ahead of them, giving them all just enough light to see where they were going.

Fritzy was just starting to feel at ease when he heard Angela yelp. He whipped around, momentarily confused as he realized that she was perfectly fine. She had her back to him and was rigid with fear. His insides froze as he saw, a split second later, that she was looking at one of the pups.

Daniel had wandered dangerously close to the edge. His front paws dug into the earth as he leaned forward, unaware of how perilously he was balanced. A small bird had captured his attention as it dove through the canyon, circling in midair.

"Daniel!" Angela screamed as he continued to bow forward. In response to the sudden shout, Daniel jumped.

The slight movement sent rocks tumbling out from under his paws. Before anyone could stop him, he was falling, head first down the side of the canyon.

"No!" Berrin was closest to the pup and he lashed out desperately, trying in vain to grab him. There was nothing the wolves could do. Time seemed to slow as Fritzy watched his son roll down the steep wall, limply slamming into the jagged rocks as he went. Angela was barking frantically as he tumbled out of sight and into the grasping darkness below.

"DANIEL!" Fritzy shouted, unable to believe what had happened. There was no way he could have survived the fall and yet he found himself calling out anyway. "Daniel!" Angela was shaking and whining. Zeke was barking, his eyes wide and shocked. The pups all gazed down at the spot where their brother had disappeared in stunned silence. Berrin was still frozen in the position he had assumed while trying to save Daniel, his mouth hanging open.

Fritzy had not the slightest notion of how long they sat there; he only knew that when they started moving again, the sun was blazing in the sky. He turned away as the light illuminated the depths of the canyon and Daniel's body lying crumpled at the very bottom. The desire he had to return to his owner was faded as though washed away by a rainstorm and a lump formed in his throat. They could not go back now; they had no territory and now they had lost a pup. Angela had been right and Fritzy hated himself for setting out in the first place. Things would have been so much better if he had simply forgotten about the boy.

Grimly now, Fritzy looked out at the horizon as they moved forward. Nobody spoke and the air was heavy with grief. He was not sure why he continued to struggle forward and he did so numbly. Thoughts of the boy swirled around in his mind, often interrupted by memories of Daniel.

Halfheartedly, Fritzy plodded on, his pack streaking morbidly behind him, the silence pressing on all of them. He licked Angela gently, telling her that things were going to be alright, though he lowered his tail guiltily, as his own words sounded strange and he was not sure if he believed them himself.

Chapter 15
Unknown Past, Uncertain Present

The next few days were difficult for the wolves, especially Angela. She would often get up in the middle of the night and go off by herself to mourn in private. Fritzy remembered waking one night to the sound of her bereaving howl, piercing his heart like Ryder's teeth had pierced his skin. He, too, missed his son greatly and sometimes, the sadness of it would threaten to overwhelm him.

Daniel, quiet, timid Daniel. The pup who- on the first day he was born- had gone straight for his father, the pup who was always ready to learn and never complained, had fallen to his death.

However, after quite a bit of time had passed, the emotional scars had healed somewhat which made it easier to travel. Fritzy's drive returned, though it was less intense than before. It was, however, enough to keep him going.

They were walking through an open field one day when Bennett began to chase Peregrine. The two jumped on one another and rolled around on the ground, snarling. Though their actions were only meant in harmless play, Fritzy suddenly realized just how big they had all grown. Even the female pups were now larger than Zeke, a fact that the wolf did not appreciate being pointed out. With a sigh, Fritzy recalled the days quite a while ago when they had been small and still relied on the pack to watch them. Berrin had always been willing to babysit and the pups preferred him as he could spin tales that would keep them captivated for hours.

Once, when Fritzy was returning from a hunt with Angela and Zeke at his side, he had heard Berrin begin to tell them his life story and the account of the fight between Fritzy, Zeke, Ryder, and the old wolf himself.

Fritzy had listened, hidden by the cover of trees, and he couldn't help but awe over what good a storyteller Berrin was. Fritzy scowled in concentration as he tried to remember what Berrin had said exactly. It had been so detailed for a cub's story. But how had it gone? Yes now he remembered...

The old wolf had peered at the puppies down his scarred muzzle, eyes glinting in the semidarkness and asked, his voice low, if they wanted to hear a story. The pups all nodded eagerly and his words had kept Angela, Zeke and himself rooted as they found suddenly that they, too, wanted to hear the tale.

"Okay," the wolf had begun, "It all started a long time ago…

"I was walking through the forest with my fellow pack members right next to me. We were on a hunt. My Alpha had recently seen a herd of elk and we were on our way to check things out. I was hungry and my stomach growled at me. I was glad- as was everyone else- when the scent of the animals finally became clear. There was another scent, too and to this day I will never forget the way it burned my nose as I breathed it in."

"What was it?" asked McKay quietly.

Berrin bent down so he was level with the pup and fixed him with a wizened and yet vice-like gaze. The moon beginning to rise in the sky reflected in the blue orbs and the wolf's voice was low and rough as he carefully pronounced the next word: "Fire." McKay gave a slight shudder. He straightened up and continued talking, his voice level now and yet as he resumed his story, it was with an air of bitter recollection.

"We were fools- all of us. As the elk came into sight, so did the fire. It rose over the trees only a few feet away. It consumed everything. I could feel the devilish heat on my face… I still wonder why I did not turn back then. Maybe it was because we were all so hungry. Maybe it was desperation that drove us forward, after the elk. They had nowhere to run and we pushed them farther back into the flames. I pursued them and- ignorant fool that I was- became lost in the fire. I could not see, I could not smell and suddenly realized that the rest of my pack had given up- that I was alone." Berrin stared up at the stars with a faraway look etched across his face. It was as if he was no longer aware of the pups' presence and was talking to someone else entirely. Himself, perhaps.

"I can remember spinning around as the fire burned closer. I panicked when it singed my fur. I had no idea where I was, and who could blame me? The smoke masked everything. I ran forward and tried to find a way through the wall of flames but there were absolutely no gaps; everywhere I turned, I was met with the same blazing heat. Someone was yelling- maybe it was me…I can't remember. Anyway, so there I was, in the middle of a forest fire and I was sure that I was going to die. The fire started catching on my fur and I ran. Just ran. The first direction I could think of was forward and so that was where I headed. By then, I could tell that the flames were eating away at me."

Star gasped. "What did it feel like?" Berrin gave a

small grunt of dry laughter, her voice bringing him back to his senses. "Surprisingly, I couldn't feel a thing. Have you ever been so desperate that you can't feel anything? Well, when that happens-" A small indignant bark interrupted him, it was Aspen.

"Who cares? Don't stop now! I want to hear what happened next!"

Berrin gave her a curt glance before resuming his tale. Fritzy had grimaced inwardly at his daughter's lack of manners and next to him, Angela had made a frustrated sighing noise. Berrin cleared his throat and opened his mouth again.

"Where was I? Oh, that's right-

"I was running much too fast and I tripped over a rock. I fell and the fire immediately reached out to me. I got to my feet as fast as I could manage and, spinning around, made a wild jump for nowhere and landed on something cold and wet. I lifted my head and realized that I had jumped clear of the fire and landed in the snow. When I saw that I was safe, the pain from my burns began to register. I don't think I have ever felt anything as agonizing as that. Patches of fur were missing and the bottoms of my paws were scorched and bleeding." The pups had winced and Fritzy sensed Zeke sway dangerously off to his left.

"I can't remember how long I was there but it was quite awhile. I could not stand because of my paws and I was about ready to give in when something amazing happened." The pups wagged in anticipation and Fritzy tensed eagerly. The old wolf looked at each of the pups in turn, the atmosphere straining under the weight of the suspenseful silence. He crouched and said, as he took a step toward Bennett, "Humans." None of the pups seemed frightened by Berrin's dramatic statement. Fritzy had smiled at that, glad that his pups had not been corrupted by the wrongful falsehood that humans were vicious killers.

Not having achieved his intended reaction, Berrin

had continued hastily. "At first I didn't know they were there- the smell of burning fur and bark masked everything- and I nearly jumped out of my charred skin when I saw one out of the corner of my eye.

"The fire had burnt down but I could still hear it crackling behind me and I turned my head slightly so I could see what was happening. I watched, pretending I was dead, as one human put out the little fire left. They looked a little burnt, too. One of them saw me and said something to his companion. By then, I was terrified."

"Why?" Daniel had interjected. Berrin looked at the brown pup quizzically. "Why were you terrified?" Daniel said, by way of clarification.

Berrin looked at him strangely and then shook his head, dismissing the comment as he chose not answer. Fritzy remembered smiling proudly then. He had made it clear to his offspring, time and time again, that humans were not dangerous and, although keeping a cautious distance was not unwise, they were not something to be especially frightened of. He had heard Angela give a quiet sigh next to him and he glanced at her. His attention changed directions, however, as Berrin recommenced his tale.

"To be honest," he had said, cocking an eyebrow, "I can't really remember much of what happened after that. I remember being moved and… I think the humans put me in some kind of fenced enclosure. I had food and water and shelter so I didn't feel that I was in a situation where complaining was necessary. I was sick and gravely injured, though and that is probably the cause for my lack of memory.

"Eventually… hmm, well, let's see… I fell asleep one day and woke up somewhere completely different." McKay raised a confused eyebrow and Berrin looked at him, innocently widening his blue eyes, "It was as simple as that. One moment I was near the humans, the next I was in the middle of an unfamiliar forest. Don't ask me how it happened because I don't know. Humans are interesting and they do so many strange things."

"Well," he went on, "I didn't know where I was but I knew one thing: I was alive and the humans had helped me. I was glad for it and I soon focused on what I was going to do next. I couldn't just sit there and let the cougars get me, could I?" The pups all shook their heads in unison, "I got up and started walking quickly. My burns were almost completely healed over which made travelling much easier," he paused as his stomach growled, "My luck ended there, unfortunately. Every pack I found would turn me away as soon as they saw me. Hunting was insanely hard because I was not powerful enough to bring down anything large. For a long time, the only thing I ate was rabbit." Peregrine made a sickened noise in the back of his throat,

"Didn't you get tired of the taste after awhile?"

Berrin laughed genuinely, "You have no idea."

"So, anyway, after awhile, I became accustomed to living alone. I hunted alone, I travelled alone and I slept alone. My only companion was the wind as it nipped at my back during the cold parts of winter. I had come to accept that there was no hope for me. I thought I'd have to wander around for the rest of my life… I was wrong of course."

Here he paused, listening to a stream gurgling nearby as the pups, and the three wolves hiding among the trees, waited impatiently for him to gather his straying thoughts. "Well…?" prompted Aspen. Berrin gave a very slight jerk and glanced around.

"Oh, oh yes. One day, I crossed a boundary line and came upon a terrible sight: three wolves were fighting. Now this wasn't the usual play fighting, mind you. This was something more serious. Two wolves were ganging up on the third and so I came to the conclusion that the third was not supposed to be there. Maybe it was my imagination running away with me but I thought he looked slightly insane. He fought viciously and with brute strength and the look he had sent chills down my spine."

A shiver had passed down Fritzy's spine as he realized Berrin was talking about Ryder. He shifted uncomfortably, sensing where the story was headed. He was not sure if he should step in with the food, ending the old wolf's story or stay hidden to hear what he had made of the event. He had decided, after a moment of pondering, to stay where he was, growling quietly at Angela as she tried to step into the open. He stiffened as Berrin's voice rang clearly out into the night.

"I recognized the scenario after a few minutes of watching. The odd wolf out was an intruder, of that much I was sure. The other two were simply trying to drive him out. Of all the times I had been denied entry to a pack, I never once argued. It was not my place and it bothered me to see this wolf fighting. I was suddenly seized with anger and, rashly, I jumped into the fight. I'll not tell you the details," Bennett looked disappointed at that, "but eventually, all of us managed to kill the rival wolf." Fritzy had glanced over at Zeke then. The gray wolf's partially concealed face portrayed a look of entertainment and a slight hint of offense. Angela sniffed and, sensing the story's end, began walking toward the group. Fritzy followed her, pretending they had only just returned. Berrin spotted them and, as his eyes fell on the food they were carrying, hastily wrapped up.

"In the end, I was accepted by the pack and we all lived together happily forever. The end." The pups looked a little confused at the sudden and unsatisfactory ending but their attention had been quickly diverted by the smell of food.

Now, as Fritzy plodded along with his family right next to him, he frowned in concentration. The old wolf had told a very interesting story and Fritzy had felt privileged by the short glance into his life. He doubted that any of his pups had understood much of the recollection at all and had a notion that Berrin had begun the story as a method of looking back into his past. The wolf's experience seemed very painful and Fritzy never would have guessed so given Berrin's good nature and polite manner. Maybe Berrin's personality was simply a way to mask his former life. The memories had to be bothersome and perhaps the wolf simply needed to talk about the happening aloud. What better audience than a group of young puppies? After all, to them, his words had appeared as a fictional scenario and half of what he had said probably didn't even register with them. They had been too young to remember the tale now. Fritzy glanced at the ground guiltily as he realized that he was prying into the other's past. He suddenly felt bad about hiding and eavesdropping and wondered if Zeke and Angela felt the same.

He glanced over his shoulder at the old brown wolf, who was walking slowly and yet steadily behind him. So, humans had saved his life? Fritzy smiled to himself realizing the reason behind Berrin's willingness to join the pack as it journeyed. Though Berrin was unaware of Fritzy's knowledge of the fact, they both knew of an unrecognized and yet real truth. Fritzy blinked and nearly tripped as something suddenly came to mind. Angela's words were ringing through his ears as walked. *"We're not just a pack of heartless monsters... We all have feelings-we all love."* This too was the case with humans, and Angela- with all her mistrustful opinions on Fritzy's owner- had stated it clearly. Wolves and humans were uncannily similar in one prominent way: they both depicted each other as murderous beasts and both opinions were equally untrue. The thought was confusing and the irony of it nearly made Fritzy laugh out loud. Angela had been the one who divulged to him the truth about wolves: they were not monsters and they were perfectly capable of love. She, however, failed to see the same truth in regards to humans. *How strange*, Fritzy thought.

Glancing at his mate, he saw that she was walking with her head low to the ground. She was still recovering from the loss of Daniel and she was no longer the happy, risk-taking she-wolf he had known. Her confidence was slowly ebbing away as was her faith in his words. Her dazzling eyes now concealed the doubt and mourning that lay behind.

He gave her an encouraging nudge as they continued their pace and made a solid and unshakable promise to himself that he would find the boy and in doing so, prove to Angela and his pack that humans were wrongfully depicted

After several long hours of walking at such a brisk pace, the entire pack was exhausted by the time Fritzy decided they needed to rest for the night. Berrin was panting, his old muscles strained. The pups were tired also and quickly situated themselves in comfortable positions in order to snag a few hours' sleep. Fritzy, Angela and Zeke- being in the best state of physical condition- suffered less than their companions but were weary nonetheless. Eventually, they found a decent place and all settled in for the night. Fritzy fell asleep quickly, mentally and physically worn.

He woke early the next morning, yawning and stretching, he sat up. Angela lay some distance off, curled into a sleeping position. The pups were scattered about, breathing deeply, Berrin lay with his head resting on his paws and Zeke was splayed nearby, snoring. Coming to the conclusion that he was the first one to arise, Fritzy looked around for the first time since they had stopped here the night before to rest.

The sun was just coming up and the sight was beautiful. He stood on the overhanging part of a very high cliff. It jutted out from the rocks and Fritzy was permitted a beautiful view from his position. Far below him was a huge lake, its shimmering surface expanded for miles before it was stopped by a barrier of thick pine trees. The rising sun sparkled in the water, its shattered reflection orange-pink.

With a sigh that was of half relaxation and half weariness, he walked over to their kill. Now that the pups were old enough to hunt sufficiently well, the hunting status had risen. The pack could now bring down much larger animals with the help of five additional sets of teeth. This time, it was a moose that would keep their stomachs from growling. Fritzy took a quick look at the carcass, noting the small pieces of flesh missing. Undoubtedly, the work of a crow.

Instead of eating, he decided to take a walk, enjoying the cool morning breeze on his face as well as the chance it provided to stretch his legs. He trotted, using his senses to almost become part of his environment. Through the pads of his feet, he felt the ground. He saw and carefully examined everything. He heard more than a half mile away, the sounds of the birds just rising to greet the day with their tweets. He smelled a rabbit not far away, but he was not interested, he was full. He tasted the air as he breathed it in. He even had a sixth sense that he was being followed and turned with a snarl to find Berrin right behind him.

The old wolf smiled apologetically. "Sorry," he said quickly. "Heard you walking away and got up."

Fritzy did not appreciate the fact that Berrin had not announced his presence. Quickly, he made a lunge for the wolf and gave him a small bite on the muzzle, a harmless warning to remind him to be more respectful next time around.

Berrin whimpered and crouched down until his belly was almost touching the ground, then he rolled over on his back and looked at Fritzy pleadingly, graciously apologizing with his entire body. Fritzy raised his head and tail in dominance and turned away, leaving Berrin to meekly scramble up.

Fritzy returned much later with Berrin by his side to find the whole pack up. He watched Angela stretch and walk over to the dead moose. The pups followed her and they began to eat. Bennett and Aspen wrestled over a piece of hide. Peregrine kept chasing McKay away from the food, barking and snarling as he nipped his brother, tail held high. Angela ate quietly until Star sneaked up behind her and barked loudly. Angela whirled around and jumped on her playfully. Bennett stopped wrestling with Aspen and walked over to the moose with his head held up proudly and the piece of hide in his mouth.

Fritzy, wagging to himself, looked away from the scene to scan the horizon. He was looking for nothing in particular, but something caught his eye. Far off in the distance, he saw something that was definitely not trees. He squinted to get a better look and his heart leapt as he realized what it was. He gave an excited whine as he recognized the shapes and turned a joyful circle. Realizing Zeke's absence, he turned to find the wolf and to inform him of his good news.

The gray wolf was sitting some distance away from the pack. He lay on a slab of rock that overlooked a vast clearing with a huge mountain in the distance. A waterfall was splashing from a river that ran directly under the rock. It fell down to land in a clear pool of water just a few feet below. Zeke surveyed the scene and watched the water rippling below his paws. Fritzy walked up behind him and gave a soft bark, for the noise of the water had prevented Zeke from hearing him. Zeke turned his head sharply and then, realizing it was Fritzy, wagged. Fritzy lay down beside his friend. There was a moment of silence and then Zeke spoke. "You seem excited; did Peregrine catch another muskrat?"

"No. I saw houses." Zeke looked up at him. His face was quite expressionless. Fritzy guessed he was trying to conceal how he really felt. "What is it, Zeke?" He asked, exasperated. Zeke pawed the rock, trying to think of how he could put into words what he thought. "The humans," he finally said, "why do you trust them?"

Fritzy opened and closed his mouth several times but he could not think of a good way to answer his friend. "There's just something special about this boy," he said. "I can sense it. He loves me and he shows it, too. It's like what you feel for a pack member. You just can't help but love them in return." Zeke gave him a bemused look. "If you knew him you'd understand," Fritzy mumbled.

"But why aren't you afraid of humans? They've hunted wolves for years." Fritzy's tail twitched in irritation, "You don't see them like I do. Wolves hunt for food and so do humans. It's not that they're destructive-they are just trying to survive."

Chapter 16
Highway

During past few days, they had covered over fifty miles. Fritzy kept them all moving, maintaining a speedy pace as he pushed forward, striving to keep the promise he had made to himself.

They began to notice traces of humans. Farmland and a few houses scattered here and there. Fritzy remembered his first glance of the city in the distance; it was closer than ever now, he could spot it whenever they crested a large hill. It was nestled among the far off trees and seemed to beckon him with a more powerful force each day.

Days came and went. Days turned to weeks, and soon they were within a day's journey. Fritzy's sense of excitement had escalated now and yet so had Angela and Zeke's nervousness. He started conversing with them cheerily to lighten their spirits. Though it seemed to help, he still noticed the anxious aura they both gave off.

The sun was just rising when the pack descended a steep, rocky incline and the wolves suddenly found themselves on a wide road. Fritzy wagged as he saw it.

The road wound its way out of sight around a bend and two rusty guardrails ran along both sides of the cement. This, however was not the reason for Fritzy's sudden wagging, for, just beyond the road and across a grassy plain, the city's many lights twinkled in the distance.

Bennett sniffed the road inquisitively, having never encountered one. Fritzy warned them all with a quiet bark to keep their distance; remembering how fast cars travelled.

Just as the thought hit him, a car sped by and they all jumped. Everyone could feel the sudden breeze on their fur as the vehicle passed and Angela whined. She had never seen a car before but it was big, fast and therefore a likely threat. She took a hasty step away from the road, her ears cocked back. Zeke's tail was quivering and Berrin was watching the car disappear around the corner with his brow furrowed. The pups came close to meeting each other's eyes, all with the same disinclined expression. Another car shot past them and this time, Zeke barked fearfully.

Fritzy stared intently at the road and then lifted his gaze to the city. A desperate longing filled him and he could not stand it any longer. Craig lived there- the boy was mere miles away. There was only one option: cross.

Glancing briefly in both directions, Fritzy stepped over the guardrail and onto the rough road. Angela growled in protest and he looked over his shoulder at her. His expression made it abundantly clear how determined he was. Angela held his gaze for half a second and then, reluctantly, began to follow.

The road was much larger than the ones he had seen and crossing it was a nerve wracking experience. The others were nervous and started frequently.

"Hurry," Fritzy hissed impatiently at them, for he could hear the rumble of a car coming in their direction, and they were only halfway across. He glanced down the road and saw something that almost made his heart stop. Speeding toward them was a large van.

"Run," he barked at them. He turned tail and headed for the other side, hoping desperately that they would make it. Relief engulfed him as his paws touched the grass on the far side and he turned around quickly, making sure the pack had made it, too. Again, he realized how lucky he was as his eyes fell on the wolves.

The van had stopped. It rested on the opposite side and Angela and the pups were dutifully making their way over to him, looking shaken. Berrin and Zeke stood in the middle, looking curiously at the car and blinking confusedly as the humans occupying it began taking pictures. Glad nobody had been hurt but still feeling rather uneasy, Fritzy gave the two a sharp, warning bark.

Pricking his ears, Zeke heard him and started the rest of the way across. Berrin glanced around for a moment and then, spotting Zeke, began following him.

Then Fritzy heard a noise that turned his blood to ice. His ear quivered as a huge semi truck barreled around the bend and headed straight for Zeke and Berrin. It was moving much too fast, it was going to hit them. There was just enough time for Fritzy to bark once before the car reached them.

Both wolves had spotted it coming at them and both bolted for the other side simultaneously. Zeke was missed by mere inches as the truck skidded in an attempt to veer around them. Berrin was a tail's breadth behind the gray wolf and, instead of simply waiting for the oncoming car to pass, panicked, running right in front of it.

After that, things almost happened too fast for Fritzy to comprehend. Zeke made it across, looking back over his shoulder as he did so. The front of the truck slammed into Berrin, momentarily catching his back legs under the tires before throwing him forward several feet with a terrible thwack. The old wolf landed on the side of the road, near the terrified pack with brutal force. For a heartrending moment, everything froze, the wind stopping in disbelief. Finally, Fritzy's mind registered it all and he sprang forward, whining. Berrin was crumpled in an awkward position and even as Fritzy drew near, he knew the wolf's injuries were fatal. He stopped and stood at Berrin's side as his pack gathered around him.

Berrin was trembling violently and he was breathing in ragged gasps. Again, the sound of Raven's dying breath flitted through Fritzy's mind and for a moment, he was unable to look at the wolf. He set his jaw and forced himself to take in the other's condition.

Blood was slowly seeping out from under him, covering the ground like a poison. Fritzy's stomach lurched as he saw Berrin's two back legs, which were twisted in the wrong direction. His muzzle had been severely scraped as it hit the pavement and bits of raw tissue were visible through the fur. Carefully, Fritzy bent and briefly licked him on the face.

As Berrin saw Fritzy, he attempted to move and gave a strangled yelp as he discovered he couldn't. Zeke turned completely away from the scene as the brown wolf fought to move. Fritzy was dimly aware of Angela's voice telling the pups to leave. None of them so much as moved. Berrin's eyes were trained on Fritzy and he ceased trying to shift. He opened his mouth slightly and gasped as he struggled to speak. Fritzy leaned closer so the old wolf's words were audible.

"F-Fritzy," Fritzy nodded stiffly.

"Yes, Berrin. I'm right here."

"I-I'm g-going to die… aren't I?"

Angela gave a quick intake of breath and Fritzy shook his head vigorously.

"No! No, your aren't going to die. You'll be fine-just hang on, Berrin."

The old wolf took a shuddering breath and looked past Fritzy into the stark sky. "It's getting darker… I can feel it…and cold."

Fritzy allowed himself a hasty glance at the humans on the road. A man had climbed out of the truck and two humans had gotten out of the van, they stood across from each other, talking quickly. The man made several shaky and apologetic gestures and they kept looking over in his direction.

"Just hold on and you'll be okay." He kept repeating this for assurance although, like calling Daniel's name had been futile, this too was hopeless. A small voice in the back of his mind was telling him that there was nothing left he could do. Berrin was too far gone to save. He took a deep breath, trying to hold himself together for Berrin's sake as the wolf continued his attempts in speaking. As he labored painfully to form the words, he was frequently interrupted by fits of wheezing and coughing.

"Fritzy," his voice was much too weak, much too gravely.

"Yes?" Fritzy could not help but whisper. Behind him, Angela was trembling.

"Come closer, I have to tell you something." Fritzy lowered his head as best he could and twitched one ear, listening fixedly. "Don't give up. You l-love that b-boy. I know humans love because-" his failing lungs forced him to stop and he lay there gasping for air for a full minute before continuing, "We…we have s-something in common, you and I. Without them… we both wouldn't… be here." He managed a weak half smile and Fritzy's tail lowered gravely. A lump formed in his throat as Berrin's eyes raked his face and then searched the air around them blindly, shuddering as another fit of coughing racked his body.

"Do you see that?" The old wolf's voice was now so weak, Fritzy had to strain in order to pick it up.

"What?" He asked, frightened. Berrin's eyes were locked on something just over Fritzy's shoulder. Turning, he found that there was nothing.

“That light. Can’t you see it? It’s so bright.” Berrin laughed which brought on more spasms. Fritzy winced as blood began to appear on his teeth, staining them red and dripping out onto the ground. Quivering, Berrin closed his eyes. His breath caught in his chest and, in one long sigh, it escaped into the air. Fritzy waited for the wolf to draw another but nothing happened. He looked as though he were asleep, still and peaceful. Fritzy swallowed hard and turned around. Berrin was dead.

Angela stood next to him, staring at Berrin’s body and trembling. She whined several times and looked up at him, her eyes swimming with grief. McKay and Peregrine stood by their mother, both looking into the distance with fixed expressions. Their siblings were a few feet off, heads low and completely silent. Zeke stood nearby, taking deep breaths, his eyes on the ground.

They stayed by Berrin's body all day and on into the night. The pups were devastated. Berrin had been a devoted and courteous pack member as well as a wonderful babysitter. They had all grown to love the old wolf. Fritzy paced for hours, thinking.

Berrin had told Fritzy about humans saving his life assuming he had not known. *“Don’t give up. You love that boy.”* Grief seemed to expand inside Fritzy’s chest. Not just for Berrin but for Daniel, as well. In an effort to get relief, he pointed his nose at the moon and howled as he had never howled before. His very soul poured out through his lips; pain, sorrow and longing all compressed into one unearthly sound. He did not stop the song until he was completely out of breath and then immediately started up again.

He howled until he was simply too tired to carry on. Numbly, he stumbled over to his mate and sat down quietly, sighing heavily.

"I can't believe this happened," he said. "I thought it was safe to cross."

"Safe," Angela said scornfully, her eyes blazing.

"There's nothing safe about humans. 'Don't worry, Angela,'" she began, imitating his words, "Everything will be okay. You just have to *trust me*.' How could you think humans love?" her voice rose, bordering on hysteria. "How could you be so FOOLISH? Moreover, how could *I* be so foolish- following you out here. I trusted you! Humans are nothing more than savage killers, who slaughter everything that gets in their way!"

Fritzy's temper flared.

"Why are you so blind," he cried. "Can't you hear yourself? As, I recall, I had that very same misconception about wolves. Who was it that opened my eyes to the truth, Angela? Furthermore, Berrin's death was not purposefully inflicted- it was an accident!" He realized he had been shouting and stopped, breathing heavily. Angela regarded him icily.

"An accident? Do think it was an *accident* that they set those traps and your foot got caught? No! They were meant to be there, meant to hurt!"

"They're just trying to survive!" He argued, "They're just like us- hunting to eat. And I got out, didn't I? We haven't seen another one since."

"'SINCE' I HAVEN'T SEEN YOU WALK WITHOUT LIMPING," Angela barked, "AND WHAT IF YOU HADN'T GOTTEN OUT? HAVE YOU EVER THOUGHT OF THAT?" She was snarling now, her teeth gleaming in the moonlight. He sensed this was getting out of hand.

Fritzy whined, "Please Angela don't yell, not in front of the pups. They'll hear you. And it's bad enough Berrin is gone without us growling at each other."

For a moment, Angela looked like she was going to bite Fritzy, then, with a heavy sigh she whispered, "You're right." Her shoulders sagged with what seemed to be the weight of the world and he suddenly grasped just how jaded she looked.

"We should all get some sleep," he said, attempting

to remove the edge in his tone. She said nothing in return, just nodded, and slunk off to find a place to rest.

Fritzy watched her go. He had no idea that journeying back home would be so hard. He wasn't even sure he wanted to keep going anymore, but the more he thought about it, the more he realized how much he needed the boy. Without him, a part of Fritzy was missing, a part that, if missing for too long, would make it harder and harder for him to live. Again, he recalled Berrin's words as he lay, dying. *"Don't give up."* Berrin would not want Fritzy to surrender. He could not leave his pack, he was as bound to them as they were to him and if he departed, the same void would open up, for nothing could replace his family.

He rested his chin on his paws and gazed at the city in the distance. It stood out against the pitch-black sky because of all the lights that had been turned on. They had made it this far hadn't they? Too tired and frustrated to think straight, Fritzy closed his eyes and fell asleep.

He dreamt he was back with his owner, they were playing and Fritzy was jumping on him like he did so often when they had been together. Then he looked over and saw Angela and the rest of the pack. They were all looking at him accusingly. They started yelling at him and Fritzy's ears began to hurt. He wished they knew what he knew. Humans were not killers, any more than they were. He tried to tell them but he couldn't shout or say anything and they kept yelling at him. The boy turned around and ran away. He looked back at his pack and instead there was Berrin on the ground, broken and bleeding. Fritzy finally found his voice and shouted.

He jerked awake and realized that he had actually cried out. He looked around him and slowly began to remember where he was and what had happened. The sorrow and the grief of the day came back to him. He wanted to howl again, to release his sorrow into the sky but instead he got up and shook himself. A noise off to the side made him jump and he turned to see Angela walking toward him.

She padded over, head and tail low in an apologetic manner, and sat down in front of him "I'm sorry," she sighed. "I shouldn't have yelled. It was wrong for me to be mad at you for loving a human. After all, love is just there like the sky, it isn't wrong to love because to love is to live. It's a part of us we cannot survive without."

Fritzy stared at her, the argument they had engaged in already seemed senseless. Of course he accepted her apology, because he loved her. It was love that kept the pack together after all they had gone through. Just like it was love that called Fritzy to return to his human owner.

He walked up to her and gave her an affectionate lick on the face. They stood close to each other and she nuzzled his neck. Love was an unbreakable bond, stronger than a leash or the fierce winds of the mountains. Stronger, in fact, than anything the world had to offer. It was then that both wolves knew:

No matter what they went through, no matter how much they suffered, they would be able to struggle through the challenges so long as they had each other.

Fritzy and Angela turned to face the city and their final destination with a solid fortitude and, gathering their pack, began moving toward it.

Chapter 17

Reunited

They covered the distance in a few short hours and soon were on the outskirts of the city. Now, all doubt was gone from Fritzy's mind. He knew with a surety that this was indeed where the boy lived, for every once in awhile, they would pass an area that was faintly familiar. Even Fritzy was somewhat reluctant to enter the city and he and his pack were careful to remain unseen. As they skirted past the buildings, it became much easier for them to move once night fell. They were still cautious, however.

Finally, Fritzy's heart raced as they came through the trees and he saw a neighborhood he recognized. Surveying the area, he thought hard, trying to remember what direction the house had been in. His instincts prompted him to go west and so he did. They had been perfectly right so far and now he felt completely secure about where they were headed.

They moved back a few yards so that they were

under the cover of trees again and took off. Angela sensed the elevated excitement in his step and allowed herself a quick wag as they took off again. They were close- he could feel it, and started running, his tail streaking out behind him and Angela by his side.

After a few heart pounding minutes, Fritzy slowed his pace and finally stopped. There it was. They were behind the houses and he recognized the backyard immediately. The house was set farther back into the trees than most others and so it was easier to see. Even at such a late hour, a few lights stood out against the darkness of the trees. Fritzy took a step forward and then stopped, cocking his head.

It was the dead of night and, from what he had learned, the humans would be asleep. He doubted he could wake them or even draw their attention to him in the dark. He would seem much too threatening. Whining, he slowly sat down, eyes fixed on the familiar scene only a few yards away. They had traveled for who knew how long, waiting one more night would not be difficult in comparison.

Zeke approached him with a confused whine, "Why are you lying down? Isn't that the house, right there?" He gave a curt nod toward the building and Fritzy looked at him.

"It's the middle of the night, Zeke. They are all sleeping."

Zeke frowned, "They sleep *all* night?" Fritzy smiled.

"Yes," he said.

Zeke shrugged and Fritzy saw him grinning- something the wolf had not done in weeks.

"This is it," Fritzy said, the relief making his words loud and happy, "This is the end."

Zeke's tail wagged and everything finally sank in. After this, there would be no more journeying, no more long days and dragging nights. No more death, no more argument. He was going to see Craig again and this was the final night of their travels.

Tomorrow, it would be over.

Where would the pack live? The question popped suddenly to mind and Fritzy realized, looking around, that he had an answer for it. Angela was talking happily to Zeke and his five pups were playing tag. They were all content and there was no longer an air of depression about them. It had vanished and it was gone from him, too.

The forest around them was large and extended far up into the mountains. There was more than enough room for them all to live here. They could stay safely out of sight and there was enough game to keep them all fed well.

Fritzy sat alone, watching his pups and smiled to himself. Last time the question had been posed, the solution had not come to him, though he had felt strangely sure that he would eventually find an answer. Now here it was. The trek had been long and confusing, now everything fell into place. His two conflicting parts- dog and wolf- were beginning to find peace. He closed his eyes and gave a long, contented sigh. Here, he could be with the boy and at the same time, lead his pack and stay with his mate. His determination and faith were beginning to pay off.

Angela walked slowly over to him. She licked his nose and sat down, leaning against his shoulder. Smiling up at him, she met his gaze and he held it. Her stunning eyes full of love and, for the first time since after the pups had been born- genuine happiness. He licked the side of her face as she buried her nose in his fur.

"We made it," she whispered, smiling. She gave a soft bark of contented laughter. "Tomorrow you'll be with your human." He wagged.

The pups rested that night but sleep evaded Fritzy. He lay awake, his heart racing anxiously, as he stared at the little house. Familiar smells were carried to him on the wind and brought back so many memories. His first day out of the adoption center, lying next to the boy's bed as he slept and finally, Craig's pained expression as Fritzy had been led away. The boy had not wanted to leave Fritzy there and Fritzy knew he had not meant to abandon him. Whatever the human had done was completely forgiven in Fritzy's eyes. After thinking this, his thoughts were immediately drawn to Ryder. The wolf had killed his father, threatened his family and nearly taken his life. Was there room for forgiveness there? And did the wolf deserve it? Fritzy scratched at a bug behind his ear. Had Zeke forgiven the wolf for the things done to him?

Out of curiosity as well as a way to pass the time, Fritzy got up to ask him. He approached Zeke and found him awake, watching a bug nearby crawl across the ground. He sat up as Fritzy drew near and yawned. "Zeke," Fritzy said, keeping his voice low, "What happened between you and Ryder?" He had not known how else to ask and wished he could have thought of a gentler way as he saw Zeke flinch at the wolf's name.

His almond eyes found Fritzy's and there was a long pause as he thought about the question. All traces of humor were gone from his face as he began speaking. "That wolf was not normal. There was always something slightly strange about him and his anger was always directed toward me. There was little I could do to defend myself because of my low rank and there were times when he attacked me." He glanced at the scar on his chest. "I got that a long time ago. He was very angry with Twilight and when I walked by, he jumped on me. I could not move as he pinned me down because he was so much bigger than me. I came away with several other cuts but *this* never healed." Fritzy had not expected Zeke to open up like this but he listened carefully as he continued.

"When you drove him out, I thought that was the end of him. I thought I'd never see him again and then he showed up in our territory. I could not stand by and let you fight him by yourself- that is why I helped you- and this time, I was stronger. I could defend myself from him."

Fritzy nodded, "So you were able to get your revenge," he said. Zeke looked at him strangely.

"Revenge? No, of course not. I fought him solely to defend my pack- I never once thought about revenge." Fritzy's tail twitched. Zeke had been defending his pack and nothing more. Fritzy wondered if things might have changed, had his mind not been distracted by fury. He had been fighting for the wrong thing and Zeke's statement was eye opening. With an understanding nod to his Beta, Fritzy turned around and padded over to his spot, his mind abuzz.

However twisted, Ryder was just another wolf and so, like any other, could be forgiven. The thought made him feel at ease and he looked at the house, his mind clearer than it had ever been.

• • •

The next day came slowly, the sun inching up above the horizon until it was settled in the sky. Fritzy began to feel slightly nervous as mid day came around- would the boy recognize him? He waited in the trees looking directly into the backyard. Everything was as he remembered it. The play structure, the veranda, the grass. Nothing had changed. He could smell the boy's scent from where he crouched and it made his heart speed. Angela shifted behind him, the entire pack clustered near, all silent and waiting patiently. He had decided that he would wait for the human to come outside before he tried to approach. They had all gained a very strong patience from hunting skittish game and so the wait was not long for anyone.

Finally, Fritzy tensed as the back door slid open and a human emerged. He stifled an excited bark as he recognized Craig. The boy was taller than Fritzy remembered and he looked older but it was unmistakably him.

He watched as the human stepped onto the grass and walked aimlessly around. Craig glanced once at the play structure but seemed uninterested. He wandered over near them and sat down on a rock, turning a stick over with his shoe then rested his chin in his hands and sat looking off into space.

Fritzy was uneasy now; he took a few quick steps toward the boy and then stopped. His nerves were getting to him. He realized he had no idea how the boy would react once they saw each other. With this thought he began to take a step backward but another feeling blossomed inside of him and he froze. It was longing. That desperate longing he had felt the whole while they were journeying. Angela brushed him with her tail and he suddenly felt less anxious.

He took a few steps and then a few more; slowly inching out from the cover of trees. Finally, he was in the backyard. The boy did not notice him and he stopped. He wasn't sure how he should approach. Half of him wanted to run up to the boy and start licking him and the other half wanted to approach slowly and quietly. In the end he let out a sharp bark.

His owner jumped at the sudden noise and looked up, startled. When he saw Fritzy he gasped and began to back away. The boy had known Fritzy as a cute German shepherd and now Fritzy was a proud and fully-grown wolf. He had changed drastically in appearance over the long months and he now looked callous and indeed, very much like a wolf.

They simply looked at each other for a moment, a boy staring directly into the eyes of a strange dog. Fritzy whined uncertainly and dipped his head. The boy squinted at him; there was something familiar about that whine, something familiar about those eyes…

Then he knew. But it couldn't be. Not after such a long time. The boy knelt down on one knee and called softly and in a nervous voice, "Here boy, come here Fritzy." Fritzy stiffened, he couldn't believe it! The boy was calling him, he remembered! Wagging furiously, Fritzy ran up to Craig, scarcely feeling his paws as they brushed the ground, and nuzzled and licked him joyously. Months of hardship fell away and he felt as though he were soaring.

Watching Fritzy so trustingly walk up to this human encouraged Angela to do so, too. Fritzy saw her out of the corner of his eye as she inched forward, head low to the ground and ears forward. He winked at her and she straightened up, proceeding in a more confident manner. As the boy saw her, he froze. Wolves did not just walk up to people like that. Angela whined and moved forward slowly. When she was close to the boy, he cautiously reached out to her. His fingertips brushed the top of her head and she almost shied away but Fritzy's look of reassurance kept her where she was. She let the boy's hand travel back behind her ears and wagged. She opened her mouth and let her tongue hang out, relaxing and showing the boy she meant no harm.

A few seconds passed, and then Zeke was there, his small form slightly crouched and his torn ear quivering. The pups were right behind him. Aspen came directly up to the boy and thrust her head under his hand. Craig laughed and stoked her, too. Fritzy watched with pride as the rest of them all approached, vying for attention. Zeke smiled as he was scratched under the chin, all doubt gone.

Soon, the pups were jumping on the boy, gently licking his face and neck. Craig was laughing under the sudden tangle of fur and noses. Fritzy wagged furiously and Angela smiled at him, a look of utter tranquility playing about her beautiful face.

The sight was strange and it marked an amazing shift in nature. Several things came together at once in that moment. Two parts of Fritzy's family were together, wolf and dog had found harmony and the gap between man and animal was sealed. Fritzy himself, was the cornerstone of the achievement. He was directly in the middle, split two ways at once. Raised by humans, living in the wild. Markings of a dog, body of a wolf. His mate sat beside him as they watched their pups playing with the human, all wagging and laughing together. Her amber eyes looked tenderly into his. Yellow and intelligent, cunning and loyal.

The eyes of a wolf.

www.ingramcontent.com/pod-product-compliance
Lightning Source LLC
Chambersburg PA
CBHW020614310726
48979CB00008B/1480/J
* 9 7 8 0 6 1 5 2 6 1 7 0 6 *